The Legend of GHASTLY JACK CROWHEART

First published in 2023 by
Andersen Press Limited
20 Vauxhall Bridge Road, London SW1V 2SA, UK
Vijverlaan 48, 3062 HL Rotterdam, Nederland
www.andersenpress.co.uk

2 4 6 8 10 9 7 5 3 1

British Library Cataloguing in Publication Data available.

ISBN 978 1 83913 309 1

Printed and bound in Great Britain by Clays Ltd, Elcograf S.p.A.

The Legend of GHASTLY JACK CROWHEART

WRITTEN & ILLUSTRATED BY

LORETTA SCHAUER

ANDERSEN PRESS

For the dread highwayman Peter,
with all my love - L.S.

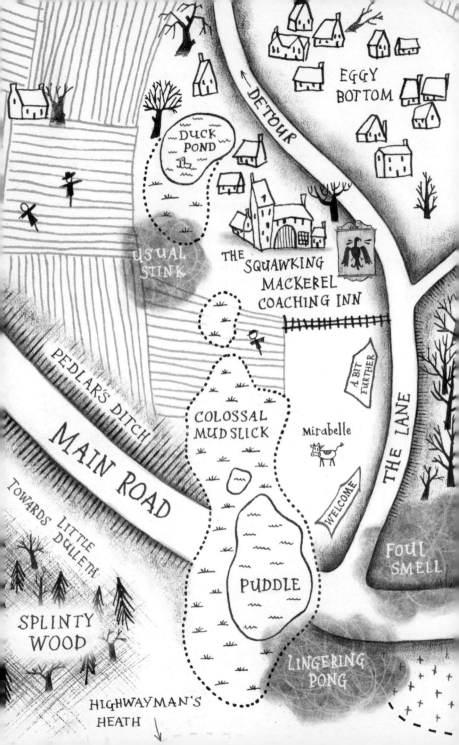

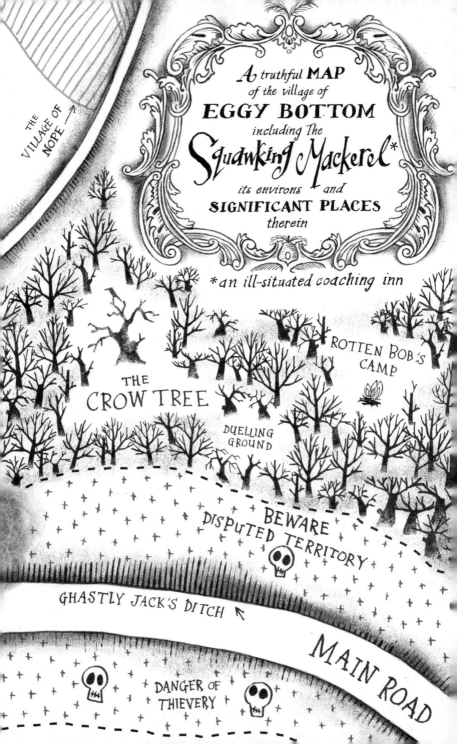

1

The Squawking Mackerel

Clank, clank, ting!

Lil ignored the bell and slopped a spoonful of greasy turnip soup into the bowl.

The old bishop took a slurp. His jowls wobbled, his eyebrows descended, and he coughed a great big glob of it out onto her foot. 'Phhah!'

'Would you like a bit of bread with that?' Lil asked, and dodged out of the way before a muddy boot landed on her backside. The Bishop was one of the regulars at The Squawking Mackerel. He wasn't the worst of Lil's customers. He did occasionally slip her a tip. A battered halfpenny if she was lucky. She sighed.

Ting, ting, clank!

'Lil! I'm busy,' shrieked her mother as she stood arranging some pickled duck toes on a platter of boiled beetroot.

'Me too,' shouted Lil's sister Margery, as she curled a lock of hair over the pimple in the middle of her forehead.

'Yeah. *Very* busy,' Lil muttered.

Leaving the basket of stale bread rolls with the Bishop, she stomped over to the entrance and stood behind the dark oak counter. As she got there, a small pale hand reached up to ring the bell again. Lil thumped the soup ladle down on the counter top and the tiny hand disappeared.

'Can I help you?' She grinned at a stooped-over gentleman in a wig. The top half of him looked as if he'd landed chin-first in a puddle.

'I *fear* you may be able to offer me a meal and lodgings for the evening,' he sniffed. 'I was told to expect the most extraordinary of welcomes by the urchin at the sign.'

'Of course, sir.' Lil scooted herself up onto the counter so she could get a better look at him. He was, after all, quite correct to fear the prospect of staying a night in this grotty place. Lil assessed how much money she was likely to be able to charge him for his stay. He had an array of oddly shaped suitcases, bags and boxes about his feet. A thin, pale boy with straw-coloured hair stood amongst them. 'How many rooms, sir?'

'One. The boy will sleep in a suitcase.'

The boy in question was certainly small. He glanced up and shrugged.

'All right,' she said, 'that'll be a shilling a night and two pennies for the boy.'

'Why should I pay for the boy if he sleeps with the luggage?'

'You'll have to discuss that with my mother,' said Lil. 'Now, why don't you find a cosy spot by the fire, and I'll serve you some hearty soup for your troubles?'

Lil was unwilling to haggle with the customers. Not her job. Leave that to Ma.

'I see that I have little choice in the matter,' snorted the gentleman. 'Be careful with those boxes, they contain my most precious inventions.'

'Inventions, sir?' Lil leaned further over the counter, all of a sudden the soggy pile of suitcases offered a glimmer of excitement.

With a flourish, the gentleman produced a damp dog-eared business card. 'I'm surprised you haven't heard of me. Mr Alwynne R. Sprottle? Purveyor of *remarkably* modern wig-warmers and . . .' he glanced around haughtily,

'. . . intimate apparel.'

'*Underwear,*' explained the boy. His cheeks flushed scarlet.

'Oh,' said Lil.

'I was on my way to Countess Hollingcroft's estate, to attend one of her exclusive soirées, when my coach was delayed by that disgraceful quagmire at Eggy Bottom. If it wasn't for that stable boy and his cow, we'd be stuck there now, sinking ever deeper into the freezing sludge.' He sniffed again, but a dribble from his nose dropped onto the front of his coat where it glistened like a slug trail. 'I'm convinced I've caught a chill.'

The only reason anyone ended up staying at The Squawking Mackerel was purely down to Lil's muck-manoeuvring efforts. There was a muddy puddle of epic proportions a quarter of a mile down the road, just before the turn-off for the inn. Sensing an opportunity to divert the coaching traffic (and penny tips) her way, Lil had blocked up the drainage ditches with mouldy cabbages, rotten turnips and leftover dumplings. The resulting mud slick ensnared even the sleekest of coaches, and by the time the stranded travellers could persuade that thick-headed oaf Arthur Boote to haul their carriage wheels out of the mess, it was usually too late for them to travel on anywhere else. So they had no choice but to arrive wet and grumpy at the doors of the inn. Tomorrow they would moan about the lumpy beds and itchy blankets, but tonight the guests were at the mercy of Ma Scroggins's cauliflower and pigeon-liver relish.

'Some soup will help with that, sir, and a nice cosy bed for the night,' Lil replied diplomatically.

'When will my room be ready?'

'A few minutes,' said Lil, cheerfully. Or rather, whenever Margery could pull her gaze away from the mirror and actually get on with some work. Margery wasn't Lil's real sister, nor was Ma Scroggins her real 'Ma'. Thank goodness.

But they might as well be. Phylis, or Lil, as everyone called her, had been 'a part of the family' for as long as she could remember. An unpaid skivvy, more like.

Lil was about to holler Margery's name when Arthur Boote exploded through the door of the inn in a blast of cold air and cow dung.

'THEY'S BIN ROBBED BLIND!' he exclaimed to a stunned room.

A barrel-bellied gentleman burst in past him, thwacking the door against the wall with a mighty crack. Some kind of lord, by the looks of him, thought Lil. Mr Sprottle tried to shuffle his precious suitcases out of the way, but the lord was oblivious as he barged into the inn, flicking dirty rainwater from his cape. He was followed by a staggering, mud-spattered lady with ringlets plastered to her face, and two bedraggled girls in soggy pink bonnets. As the lady realised she'd reached dry ground, she swept her arm above her head, placed the back of her hand upon her brow and declared, 'The horror!' She then collapsed to the floor in a dead faint.

The room erupted.

Gentlemen rose to their feet in outrage. 'Madam!? Sir!? My very goodness!'

Ladies fluttered their fans in sympathy.

Clearly, neither the lord nor the lady was blind – but they had indeed been robbed.

'He was a savage fiend!' exclaimed the lord.

'*Savage*,' confirmed Arthur.

'He manhandled my manservant, and looted our trunks!'

'*The devil*!' (Arthur again.)

'He rifled our pockets, bold as brass, with his own fi*lthy* mitts!'

'*Nasty man*,' Arthur nodded.

Ma Scroggins had rushed over to administer to the lady, who had collapsed into a puddle of her own silks. Her wig had popped off in the commotion so Ma shoved it back on her head, though it might have been back to front.

'What did he look like?' asked Ma, shocked.

'About six feet tall,' the lord continued.

'*A giant*,' added Arthur.

'He was unshaven and grubby. He had the most terrible dark twitchy eyes and a most unpleasant . . . fetid . . . er . . . ' He screwed up his nose and wiggled his fingers in search of the right word.

'He stank of cheesy feet,' peeped one of the little girls.

'The whole lot of them did,' added the other.

'*Highwaymen*!' declared Arthur.

The man turned to Ma Scroggins and fixed her with an entitled glare. 'We will obviously require accommodation.'

'Well, I might be able to make one of our more exclusive rooms available . . . it'll cost ya, though.'

'Madam!' the man gasped. 'We have been burglarised! Would you take advantage of a family forced into such dire circumstances? I am shocked and appalled!'

Ma Scroggins pulled herself up indignantly.

'Well, I don't mean to be impolite, sir, but I've got a business to run 'ere.'

'How could you demand payment in light of a predicament such as ours? In fact it is an insult. Do you know who I am?'

Ma Scroggins shuffled and frowned. Had she missed something? 'I'm sure we could come to some arrangement . . . but this is a much sought-after establishment . . .'

'Madam! My wife, my daughters and I have experienced a most vicious attack, inflicted upon us by a bunch of merciless scoundrels and we will not be *further* inconvenienced by *your* daylight robbery. We will require a suite of rooms. There is my family of course, our immediate staff and footservants, plus the coaching attendants. We'll take the entire first floor. I trust you are able to accommodate a family of our standing in the manner to which we are accustomed?'

Now it was Ma Scroggins who turned pale and started to stagger.

'I . . . I'm sorry, sir, we are almost full-to-bursting this evening!'

The man's face turned a thunderous shade of purple. A vein throbbed on his forehead. But he replied in a clear, slow voice.

'My good woman, I am the fourth EARL OF ROCHESTER!'

Well, that changed everything.

Ma Scroggins shuddered to attention and began spluttering apologies and platitudes.

Rooms were to be made available. Paying guests were to be inconvenienced. Fuss was to be made and escalated in proper proportion to Rochester's rank and status. Naturally, the requirements of an earl trumped those of any other customer who had suffered the misfortune of winding up at The Squawking Mackerel that night. A troop of wet and muddy servants marched through the inn, rearranging furniture and commandeering everything from blankets to bed pans. Everyone was obliged to make way – all except

the old bishop, who sat there rumbling into his soup. Nobody dared budge a bishop.

'Welcome to The Squawking Mackerel,' Lil muttered. 'Possibly the mizzliest, bleakest little coaching inn on the edge of nowhere interesting, in the middle of the Great Long Boring Road between Snottingham and London.'

Ma would be furious at having to put up all these extra guests for free. The sensible thing for Lil to do would be to keep a low profile until Ma calmed down.

Remarkably Modern Bloomers

L il surveyed the dining tables, looking for the next crisis to avert. She noticed a gaggle of ladies had settled themselves around one wonky table, and a cluster of gentlemen had arranged themselves at another. Despite their expensive silk and furs, they all looked like someone had poured a bucket of Eggy Bottom pond water over their picnic. Feathers had limped, rouge had run, and pomade had slipped to form a crackly rim at the edges of their perfectly powdered foreheads.

Mr Sprottle had wasted no time in swooping in on the pair of middle-aged ladies nearest the fireplace, who half listened to him with a look of mild distaste upon their

bedraggled faces. His sales pitch on 'Remarkably Modern Bloomers' and self-scaffolding undergarments had not gone down well. Now he had artfully arranged a selection of buttons, trinkets and ribbons on the table in front of them.

'I can assure you that they are all the rage on the Continent. Although Countess Hollingcroft *herself* was particularly interested in my *panniers.*' Sprottle produced a tattered pamphlet from his soggy pocket. 'One can never have *too* expansive a skirt this season, provided one has the *vast* doorways and a *big enough* residence to accommodate such fashion of course, ho, ho,' he tittered.

Lil frowned. She'd never heard of panniers. But at the

mention of the countess's name, the ladies' interest was suddenly piqued. Lil sidled closer to the conversation. The woman on the panniers pamphlet looked like she had a couple of baskets stuffed under her petticoats to make her dress stick out at the sides. Lil wondered what would happen when she tried to sit down. And she'd have to shuffle sideways through doors.

Several linen items in Sprottle's boxes had got damp in the downpour. The boy stood with his arms outstretched by the fire while Mr Sprottle proceeded to arrange items on him like a drying rack, all the while chattering away at his customers.

The boy sneezed.

'I do beg your pardon, ladies, one of the *downsides* of a portable clothes rack...ho, ho.'

Sprottle turned to bark at the boy, 'Fetch the other pannier pamphlet. Quickly. From the bag.' He then turned back to the lady on his right, tapping the side of his nose theatrically. 'An exclusive preview of this season's *must-have* silhouettes...'

Achieve the most

E-X-P-A-N-S-I-V-E

silhouette, with

A R SPROTTLE's

SUPERIOR

SELF~SCAFFOLDING

dignified   secure

PANNIERS

Be prepared with Sprottle's

PATENTED EVER-EXPANDING DESIGN

3

Shiny Things

U p in the rafters, two beady black eyes watched the scene below. A great flock of humans had squeezed themselves into the inn that night. They squawked and flapped and made a mighty clatter as they came inside to roost!

There was a great big noisy one, waving and bellowing, and lots of nervous ones who were scurrying about making a comfy nest for him. Even Ma Scroggins did as she was told when the big one barked.

The watcher had not stolen anything from them. Not yet. He waited for them to settle.

A chattering newcomer produced several shiny treasures

from a small
box, and spread
them on a table
in front of some
fancy feathery ones.
He was showing off:
'Chitter, chitter,
chitter,' he went. But the
fancy feathery ladies pretended
they weren't impressed.

The watcher peered at the shiny treasures
with one eye, then the other.

He watched as a small scrawny boy crouched under the
treasure table, searching, rummaging.

The watcher hopped to the floor.

Something brushed against Lil's ankle. She glanced down to
spot a small black scruffy bundle hopping under a chair. It
sat there, eyeing up the trinkets on the table. Lil stamped her
foot, but the beady-eyed bird just sauntered closer to where
the clothes-rack boy crouched under the table, digging
into a bag.

CAAAAAW!

The boy jumped up and hit his head on the underside of the table, sending the trinkets and buttons flying, along with several bowls of lumpy soup. Some of which splattered across the gown of one of Mr Sprottle's potential customers. She sat bolt upright, blinking a piece of parsley out of her eye while Mr Sprottle leaped to his feet and began wafting a napkin at her.

'I'm so sorry. Such clumsiness,' he yelped.

Quick as a flash, the cawing ball of feathers swooped in, grabbed a shiny button off the floor, and flew into the coal bucket near the fire.

'Aaaargh! What was that?' yelled Lady Pilchington-Whare, squinting through her good eye.

'What was what?' Lil asked innocently.

'Was it a crow?'

'No! I don't know. It wasn't a crow.'

'Not a crow?'

'It was definitely a not-a-crow, m'lady!'

'You *silly* boy! Those silver buttons cost three shillings
each!' bellowed Sprottle.

Lil darted towards the fireplace. 'Just adding some more
coal to the fire,' she muttered, snapping the lid of the coal
bucket tightly shut. She gave it a good shake until something
metallic rattled inside. Nobody took any notice of Lil. They
watched, agape, as Mr Sprottle hopped from foot to foot
fretting about the soup stains, and the boy frantically dabbed
at the wet patch on Lady Pilchington-Whare's gown.

Lil lifted the lid of the coal bucket and a dishevelled tail-
less crow shot out and sat on the window ledge, trailing a
cloud of soot. She reached into the bucket.

'Here's a button!' she called, rushing up to the table. 'Let
me sort that out for you, m'lady . . .'

'What's going on over 'ere?' Lil's mother barged her way
through the tables. 'Lil? Is that you causing trouble? Is that
pesky bird in 'ere again?'

'No, Ma, just helping Lady Pilchington-Whare. There's been a soup incident.'

Lil risked a glance at the windowsill. Augustus Scratchy, the crow, had flown out, leaving two sooty scuff marks behind him.

'I'm so sorry, Lady Pilchington-Whare! Do forgive me,' warbled Mr Sprottle.

'Here now, why don't you go up and change, Lady P? Give that dress to Lil and she'll 'ave it clean by the morning,' said Ma Scroggins. 'Margery! Come and see if the ladies and gentlemen would like something else to eat or drink. I 'ave a delicious jellied trout and minced crabapple pie that's just come out the oven,' she crooned.

Margery humphed past, kicking a broken crock of soup and grinding its contents into the rug. 'Scrawny little bog beast,' she hissed at Lil.

Lil scooped up the broken crockery and started to mop up the soup. She was sick of Margery. Why did she always have to make things worse? It was Margery's belief that one day she would catch the eye of a fine gentleman and be whisked away from her life of drudgery to live in a nice posh house. Lil thought it more likely that Margery would marry Arthur Boote.

Arthur lived next door at the Eggy Bottom blacksmith's with his dad and his gormless sister, Maude. Arthur was a smug-faced little snitch, who could never keep his mouth shut. It was his job to lurk about the inn sign, hauling wagons out of the mud with his pet cow Mirabelle. His dad, Mr Boote, was always sniffing around the inn, proposing various 'business arrangements' to Ma. And Maude? Well, Maude was Margery's *best friend*. Although goodness knows why – she was so boring. Margery and Maude were experts in petty gossip and slack-mouthed dawdling, and

they *never* missed an opportunity to pick on Lil. She hated the lot of them.

After the shifting and shunting of guests and rooms, it was clear that Mr Sprottle had drawn the short straw and was dumped into a tiny room in an annexe. There was barely enough space for the bed, so it was agreed that some of his suitcases and boxes would have to be stored elsewhere, guarded by the boy. Lil stacked them outside the lost property cupboard.

She was curious about the clothes-rack boy.

'What's yer name?' she asked.

The boy stared at her in silence for a few moments before replying.

'Um . . . Ned. I mean, Snederick Smythe really, but everyone calls me Ned. Well . . . they don't really, they call me "Boy" usually . . . But I'm Ned.'

He nodded as if he'd just convinced himself.

'Well, Ned, make yourself comfy. There's a sack of quilts in the corner. They're probably clean as they've never been on the beds in this place. Just a bit dusty – give them a thump. That's it. I'm Lil, by the way.'

She nodded towards the open cupboard.

'Thank you, Lil,' said Ned. He stared at Lil again for a

few moments, then climbed in on top of the quilts and crossed his legs. 'I've never had my own room.'

'Well, make the most of it. Here's a candle, don't fall asleep and forget to blow it out.'

'I won't,' he replied eagerly.

'Goodnight, then.'

Ned sat amongst the lost property as if he had just been crowned king of the cupboard.

'Goodnight . . . thanks!' He waved.

Lil shook her head and bustled off to the kitchen to grab a mug of milk to take up to her own attic room. 'Odd boy,' she muttered to herself.

4

Augustus Scratchy

Early the next morning, Ned was standing beside the door to the lost property cupboard. He was so still, Lil nearly walked past him. She stopped and grinned. 'Good morning.'

'Thank you. For last night, I mean. Finding the button and everything...' he stammered. 'And for letting me sleep in the cupboard... Sorry, I'll get out of your way.'

He slunk back, pressing himself into the wall.

'You're not in my way,' Lil replied gently.

Ned peered up at her. A smile broke across his freckly face.

'So... What are you up so early for, Ned?' she asked.

Everyone else at the inn was snoring and it was still dark.

'Me? To see if I can be of service. I have to anticipate Mr Sprottle's needs, and make myself useful at *all times.*'

'Sounds boring,' Lil scoffed.

Ned giggled. 'Yeah, emptying his chamber pot and picking nits out of his wig, mostly.'

Ned pretended to flick fleas off the end of his thumb.

'I'm a *temporary* solution for Mr Sprottle,' Ned declared, mocking Mr Sprottle's *dealing-with-a-bothersome-person* voice. 'Once his inventions become famous, I shall no longer be required.'

'Ha! Me too. I'm only here temporarily.' Lil grinned.

Ned frowned.

'I have plans to see the world before I'm twelve,' she explained.

'I've seen quite enough of it,' said Ned. 'I'd rather stay here in the lost property cupboard.'

Lil laughed again . . . but she suspected Ned was being serious.

'Anyway, I'd better go and see if Mr Sprottle is awake . . .'

'He's sound asleep. There's not been a peep out of any of the guests yet. Come and help me load up the turnips instead.' She nudged Ned's foot. 'Come on, I'll show you something.'

'I don't want to get in any trouble.'

'You won't. Come on.'

With a nervous grin, Ned followed Lil through the kitchen, and out of the back door to the turnip shed. It was Lil's job to fetch in the turnips at the start of the day and to load up the rotten bits of turnip peel

and kitchen waste in the wheelbarrow at the end of the day. She was supposed to dump the leftovers in the stinking rubbish pit behind the stables, but she had been secretly wheeling most of them out to the drainage ditch at the end of the lane instead. Lil was in sole charge of turnip transportation at the inn and no one poked their nose into her territory.

It was chilly outside, and the turnip shed smelled of damp soil and rotting root vegetables. There was a croak from the shadows. Ned froze, grabbing Lil's arm.

'It's that weird crow from last night. In the coal bucket,' he whispered.

'The very same,' Lil smiled proudly. 'Ned, meet Augustus Scratchy. I rescued him from the cat when he was a baby.'

'What happened to his tail?'

'The cat,' said Lil.

Augustus Scratchy cawed loudly.

'Will it grow back?' asked Ned.

'I don't know,' said Lil.

'Can I stroke him?'

'Yeah. He's friendly. Mostly. But be careful, he'll have a go at your hand if he thinks he can get away with it. He forgets *I saved his life.*'

This last comment Lil directed at Scratchy, who was perched on the handle of a turnip shovel, peering at Ned through one eye, then the other, assessing whether to screech and snap his beak or to behave like a gentleman and accept being stroked.

Ned withdrew his fingers, and took a step back.

'He's...um, fierce,' he said.

'Ma won't allow him in the inn, but he gets in anyway. He's responsible for half the lost property in the lost property cupboard. He "lifts" stuff from guests, if you know what I mean? Because of his tail, he can't fly very well, and I've told him the cat will nobble him again one day, but I think he likes taunting it. I like him.'

Ned didn't have anything to say to that, so they stood there in silence for a bit until Ned started to shuffle and look back at the inn.

'I should go. I'll get in trouble if Mr Sprottle is calling for me and I'm not there.'

'All right,' Lil said. 'But don't tell anyone about Scratchy. It's a secret. Especially not Margery, Maude or Arthur Boote. They're not to be trusted, you understand?'

'I won't say anything,' replied Ned. 'I'm just a walking clothes rack.' Ned winked, grinned, and scuttled back to the inn.

Lil liked Ned too.

5

Highway Robbery and the Turnip Apocalypse

B reakfast was being served, and the usual complaints were being aired, when the next batch of burglarised travellers banged on the door of the inn.

They'd been held up by highwaymen too.

The Offington-Minors had been relieved of their valuables by a mob of masked robbers who appeared to be led by someone called 'Rotten Bob'. The Toffyngton-Tweedes had been molested by a gang of hoodlums who had swept upon them from the nearby woods and ruthlessly stolen their brooches, bracelets and bonnets. Most distressing

of all, Miss Eloisa Primp had had her purse plucked from her person and been made to *walk* through the mud. She had not fared well during the experience. Her silken slippers had disintegrated and her delicately embroidered gown had become so weighed down with muck that she could only shuffle forward, leaving a trail of sludge behind her. Someone had perched her on the edge of a settee with a bottle of smelling salts.

The inn was a hive of activity, but to Ma Scroggins' dismay, none of the new guests had any money left. Not even a scrap of jewellery. Yet here they were, arriving on her doorstep in varying degrees of misery, demanding refreshment, and clogging up the tables. The paying guests were hurrying swiftly about their business, unwilling to linger in such a dangerous neighbourhood. Ma was stuck with an inn full of whinging customers who were all skint.

'I shall be ruined,' she wheezed as she plonked a cold compress on an elderly woman's head. The woman whimpered and began warbling about her lost earrings.

Ma wiped her hands on her filthy apron and shook her head.

'At this rate I shall 'ave to sell up and move out.'

Mr Boote, Arthur's dad, sat on one of the inn stools

helping himself to the pickled duck toes left over from the previous evening. 'T'aint much better at the blacksmith's. I reckon we wanna throw in our lots together, Ma Scroggins, and invest in a turnip farm. The kids could work it, and we wouldn't 'ave to worry about no moanin' customers nevermore again.'

'Another few days of this lark and I might just take you up on the offer!' Ma complained. She put her hands on her hips. '*Ma Scroggins' Turnip Pies*. It has a nice ring to it. Lil and Arthur could do the digging. Margery and Maude could sell pies in town.'

Lil felt the blood drain from her face. There was no way she was prepared to spend her life digging up turnips with Arthur Boote. If she could imagine anything worse than working at The Squawking Mackerel that was probably about it! And how would she earn tips on a turnip farm?

'Nobody eats turnips if they can help it, and your pies are horrible,' she mumbled.

'What did you say?' shouted Ma.

'Nothing,' Lil called back. 'Just going to mop up out the back.'

EXTRA TEA
2 shillings

Lil didn't know why the highwaymen were picking off the inn's customers all of a sudden, but she *did* know she wasn't going to end up digging turnips in a field. She needed to find out more about these dastardly thieves, so she slunk over to the table in the back parlour where a group of grizzled coachmen sat with their feet up, slurping tankards of ale.

'Sounds like you've had quite a morning,' Lil said, picking up an empty ale pitcher and wiping away the soggy patch underneath it.

''Orrible morning,' agreed one of the carriage drivers. 'I've never seen it so bad.'

'You couldn't go two hundred yards without some chancer racing up to the coach and shouting "Stand and deliver!"' said another. '"We ain't got nothing *left* to deliver," I says, "we been cleaned out by your mates already, back round the corner!"'

They all chuckled at this.

'What do you think's brought 'em all out the woodwork then?' asked Lil.

The first coachman shook his head. 'It's that bloomin' great puddle that's done it. It slows the coaches down and makes us easy pickings for the highwaymen. It was bad

enough getting stuck in it, but now the puddle's got so big you get robbed into the bargain!'

There was lots of nodding and tutting.

'I got held up three times on the same run this morning!' said another coachman. 'Used to be able to crack the whip and keep your speed up, and if the robbers didn't like the look of you comin' fast at 'em, they'd leave you alone,' he complained. 'Now they're like a pack of vultures!'

'They're all picking over the same little patch of road, that's the trouble.' This coachman was the oldest, and his hands were weathered and gnarled. He stretched back in his seat as he explained. 'Y'see, cos of that bloomin' great puddle, we all drive up round Eggy Bottom now and we don't rejoin the *main* road again until right up near Little Dulleth. That puddle's knocked out all their usual haunts, seein' as nobody goes past Pedlar's Ditch or Splinty Wood any more.'

'Yeah and they're vying for territory now. Getting quite vicious too!' a chubby faced post-boy interrupted. 'That puddle's upset a proper hornet's nest, it has!'

The coachmen and carriage drivers didn't seem in any great hurry to get on with their journeys as they sat around discussing the recent surge in highway robbery. Lil was certain they'd be charging their passengers extra time for the delay too. The older chap put his tankard down and burped loudly.

'Used to be a gentlemanly trade, highwaymanning. Not any more, if this lot's anything to go by.'

'What makes you say that?' Lil asked.

The old coachman shook his head. 'Right *rough*-looking bunch, this lot... nevermind the fancy boots and... gaudy hats...'

'Rotten teeth and foul language, more like!' interrupted another. 'That big blighter, wos 'is name? Bob Hatchet? The stench when he pulled off his kerchief to shout at us! One waft of that and I thought my 'orses was going to faint!'

They all laughed again and smacked their tankards together.

It was all her fault!

Lil's plan had redirected travellers to the inn, but it had also displaced the local highwaymen, forcing them to

converge on the stretch of road just before the inn. With the drainage ditches blocked, the massive puddle she'd created must have grown and joined up with Eggy Bottom's duck pond. Apparently, the road was now impassable without a small boat. It had seemed a good idea at the time; get rid of the leftovers, and encourage a bit more business their way. But Ma's dumplings were like rocks at the best of times, even worse when they were stale! What if the blockage was permanent? She needed some kind of giant plunger before anyone found out what she'd done!

'Lil! What are you up to over there? There's no time for idle chatter!'

'Coming, Ma!' Lil grabbed the empty jug and slung the cloth over her shoulder.

'Listen.' Her mother stood with her hands on her hips and the grotty tea towel screwed up in her fist. 'The earl

and his *delightful* family are leaving now.' She glanced across to one of the earl's footmen, who was struggling out of the door with three overstuffed suitcases. He appealed for someone to help him. Ma tutted and looked away. 'So you'd better get up them stairs and strip all the rooms. I want everything back in its proper place. Empty the chamber pots, swill out the wash bowls, and sweep the floors. Those rugs are going to need a beating too. So many muddy feet tramping in and out last night. Anyone would think I kept a pigsty, the mess upstairs! Have a sniff of the sheets and give the dirtiest ones to Margery out in the yard. The rest can be straightened out and kept on the beds for the next lot of freeloaders we get dumped on us.'

'I've got all my other jobs to do as well, Ma!' Lil was racking her brains on how to unblock a ditch.

'Ain't we all? Everyone's gotta pull their weight!'

'Yeah, looks like me doing all the pulling from this end,' she muttered. 'What's Margery doing?'

'Your *sister* is outside doing the laundry with that dear girl Maude.'

'So . . . standing about gossiping about boys, you mean?'

'Leave her out of it, and get about your own business. I've had enough of your cheek, young lady! I've got a busy

day seeing to all these customers, and I don't know when I'm going to find the time to prepare tonight's menu. I'd been planning another little experiment with pigeon livers, but I shan't have time at this rate. It'll be leftover dumpling surprise and they'll 'ave to like it or lump it. That reminds me, Lil, you'd better stick them dumplings in to soak for a bit.'

'Why bother?' Lil should have kept her mouth shut, but as Ma stood in stunned silence, she couldn't help herself. 'Those dumplings will be like bricks whether they're soaked or not!'

Ma's face washed scarlet. She sucked in a breath, ready to send a blast of fury in Lil's direction.

To Lil's relief there was a loud cough from the stairs and Ma Scroggins spun round to snap at whoever'd dared interrupt her.

It was Mr Sprottle. The inn's only paying guest.

Ma's expression transformed like a wave retreating over a pebbly beach.

'Oh, good morning, Mr Sprottle,' she beamed. 'Did you sleep well?'

Mr Sprottle looked grey and watery and was clutching a snotty handkerchief to his chest.

'Not at all,' came the terse reply. 'I demand to be moved to a more suitable room.'

'Oh? You'll be staying another night, then?' Ma fluttered her eyelashes and clasped her hands in front of her apron. Lil took her chance to sneak up the stairs.

'I appear to have contracted a chill. An evening spent enduring a muddy deluge, followed by a night in a mouldy box room has gone straight to my chest. Alas, I am too unwell to travel today.'

Lil paused her dash up the stairs and leaned over the bannister to listen.

'Oh dear, Mr Sprottle, you poor thing. Well . . .' Ma took a step closer to Mr Sprottle, 'between you and me, now that Earl wots-'is-features has shifted out, we can move you to a room more befitting your circumstances. Once Lil has sorted the rooms, she'll move you into the *Royal Suite* so you can recover in comfort.'

The Squawking Mackerel didn't have a Royal Suite. No royalty had ever stayed, nor ever *would*, stay at the inn. But

Ma had a knack for sniffing out those customers with an inflated idea of their own importance. The 'Royal Suite' was one of the larger rooms on the first floor, with a cupboard for the privy, and a washstand by the window.

'Once you get settled in I'll make you a nice cup of medicinal tea. My own special recipe passed down from my dear old mother. Very good for the sinuses and the digestion. That'll sort you out. I'll have your boy bring it up to you.'

'Looks like we'll be staying after all.'

Lil turned to see Ned standing behind her, peering over the bannister as well.

'At least we have one paying customer willing to spend a couple of nights here.'

'I can give you a hand with everything once Sprottle's settled into his new room. He'll fall asleep with a sprig of mint strapped to his forehead – he reckons it helps ward off diseases. And then I can come and help you in the turnip shed again.'

Lil sighed and slumped back from the bannister. 'Any good at unclogging ditches?'

'I doubt there's much anyone can do about that. Not until it stops raining!' Ned shook his head. 'You'll have to wait until the waters subside.'

'It might be too late by then.'

'Well, it's hardly your fault. Something must have blocked it up over the summer.'

Lil was silent.

'At least it's bringing customers to your inn,' Ned continued cheerfully. 'We would never have turned off the main road if it wasn't for that puddle blocking the way.'

'Yes, but now everyone who turns up has been robbed, so it doesn't do us any good, does it? It can't go on like this,

Ned. If I can't get rid of the puddle, I've got to find some way of getting rid of these highwaymen. Apart from all the extra work, Ma's threatening to sell the inn and move us to a turnip farm!'

'Would that be so bad?'

'YES!' Lil raised her eyebrows. 'I don't want to live on a turnip farm. It would be a *disaster*. No one would want to buy Ma's horrible turnip pies and then where would we be? Plus they'll make me get rid of Scratchy! They won't want him picking around the farm, and Mr Boote hates him. He says crows are bad luck.' She slapped the bannister angrily. 'Those highwaymen are ruining everything.'

6

WAR!

Out in the fields, alongside the road, Augustus Scratchy was spying on the Nasty Faces.

That was what the big crows called the highwaymen, and today the Nasty Faces were stealing shiny things from all the fancy folk who wore someone else's feathers and didn't do their own walking.

Another coach full of passengers rattled to a halt. The fine horses snorted and nodded their heads as the rich occupants were forced to step out onto the muddy verge.

'If I were as big as those great big horses,' Scratchy thought, 'I wouldn't pull them. And I certainly wouldn't let them ride on my back. I'd run off, kicking the dirt in their faces.'

But as he watched, the horses stood still and the Nasty
Faces swaggered about, flapping and yelping at the coach
party until they handed over their treasures.

Some of the fancy feathered ones were far bigger than
the Nasty Faces. Scratchy wondered why they didn't just sit
on them and give them a good pecking until they gave back
all the shiny things they had taken.

He spotted another crow observing the scene. She was
waiting for her chance to nip in and steal something for
herself. She stalked up and down the path near the Nasty
Faces, peering out of one eye, then the other, watching for
the right moment to pounce. Three more of the big crows

joined her on the ground. They hopped in for a closer look, then hop-skip-flapped away whenever the humans looked at them.

The big crows had clashed with the Nasty Faces before. They knew the shabbily dressed men were aggressive and mean. The crows would not tolerate the Nasty Faces in their territory.

The first crow darted closer, but one of the Nasty Faces kicked at her. She cawed and flapped away.

By now there were more crows perched in the surrounding trees. A big old male with a sleek black head shouted: *'CAW! CAW! CAW!'*, calling out the threat as he would for a marauding hawk or rival flock. More and more reinforcements arrived. Suddenly, at the big crow's signal, there was a swirl of black feathers and dozens of crows swooped in to fight.

It was war.

The Nasty Faces flapped and squawked, protecting themselves from the snapping beaks and scratching claws. The fancy humans clambered back into their coach and flicked at the horses, desperate to get away. Scratchy stood on a fence post to join in

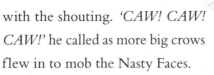

with the shouting. *'CAW! CAW!*
CAW!' he called as more big crows
flew in to mob the Nasty Faces.

As the crows were beginning to
hammer home their numerical advantage, a tall
grimy man strode out of the woods. He pulled down
the stained neckerchief that covered his mouth and
stood at the edge of the road with his hands on his hips and
a snarl on his rough grubby face. He looked like one of the
Nasty Faces, but his expression was far meaner.

'GEEROUTTAVIT!' he yelled, but no one, neither crow
nor human, took any notice. He picked up a rock and threw
it. Then another. Still there was no response as the crows
swooped and pecked and the Nasty Faces yelped and flapped.

Finally he took a big stick thing from his
belt and pointed it at
the crows.

BANG!

Instantly, the crows flew up as a great shrieking black mass. They soared up to the sky and scattered into the trees.

Scratchy scooted under the nearest hedgerow in fright.

The Nasty Faces then gathered up their hats and slunk into a subdued herd, as smoke drifted across the road from where the stick had gone bang.

Scratchy crouched silently in the scrubby branches, and watched.

The big stinker roared at them, his scuffed boots clanking in the gravel as he stalked up and down. He was clearly in charge and he was angry. He gave each of the other Nasty

Faces a handful of flappy white leaves and some shiny little thorns. He snapped and growled at them once more, then stomped back into the woods the way he'd come. The Nasty Faces wandered off, muttering amongst themselves and sticking the flappy white leaves to tree trunks and fence posts with the shiny thorns.

When they had gone, Scratchy hopped closer to one of the leaves to investigate. It had marks scrawled across it like footprints. He picked at it with the tip of his beak. It wasn't food, but it was pleasantly crinkly, and the little thorn glinted in the sunlight. He gave it a sharp tug and it came away in his beak. He would take it as a gift to the little one who shared her food with him.

Stinging Hankies

When Lil entered the yard carrying a vast pile of dirty sheets, Margery was standing knee-deep in a tub of soapy water. 'Doing the laundry' mostly meant Margery and Maude flapping the odd sheet about and treading it in the tub whilst chatting about boys. Most of the sheets sat in the basket, growing mouldy.

'Here's another batch!' chimed Lil, dumping an armful of sheets into the tub where Margery stood with her skirts tucked into her bloomers so as not to get them wet. Lil chucked in a couple of Mr Sprottle's snotty hankies on top. She'd assured Ned that Margery wouldn't mind her adding them in with the whites, seeing as she was doing a load anyway.

'Oi! Don't splash! And what's that? I'm not touching those. Get 'em outta there!' Margery scooped up the soggy pile, hankies and all, and shoved them back at Lil, soaking her with dirty water. 'I've been slogging away all morning and I don't have time for you to be dumping your chores on me as well!' Margery stomped out of the tub, and shoved Lil and the soggy washing backwards into a patch of stinging nettles. Lil stumbled and tried to save herself, but with her arms full she landed on her behind with a yelp. The nettles stung her legs

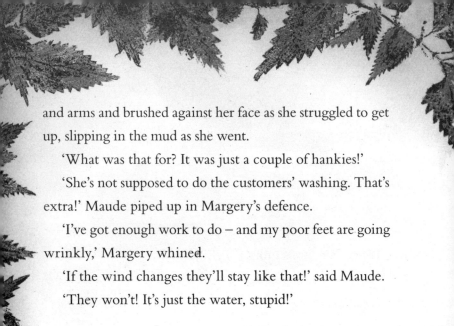

and arms and brushed against her face as she struggled to get up, slipping in the mud as she went.

'What was that for? It was just a couple of hankies!'

'She's not supposed to do the customers' washing. That's extra!' Maude piped up in Margery's defence.

'I've got enough work to do – and my poor feet are going wrinkly,' Margery whined.

'If the wind changes they'll stay like that!' said Maude.

'They won't! It's just the water, stupid!'

'Don't you call Maude stupid, stupid!' snapped Margery.

'Well, you've got to do them other sheets anyway.'

'Get them out the mud then, you filthy little imp, you're making them worse!'

Lil gathered up the scattered laundry, dumped it in the dirty basket, and slunk off behind the turnip shed to look for a dock leaf. The stinging nettles had hurt. Her legs, arms and face were coming up in red welts and she wanted to cry. She wouldn't let Margery or Maude see her though.

She kicked about in the weeds that marked the edge of the veg plot. The long wet grass soaked the mud off her ankles and felt cool and clean. She was lost in a familiar fantasy where she was waving goodbye to the inn from the top seat of a coach, all packed up and ready to go exploring the Americas, when Scratchy flapped up to the top rung of the fence to greet her. His customary *'CAW!'* was muffled by a piece of paper in his beak.

'Whatcha got there, Scratchy? Let me look.'

He hopped from side to side before letting Lil catch hold of the paper, then flapped up to the shed roof with a loud *'CAAAW!'*

It was a notice.

I, Rotten Bob Hatchet (Chairman), in ~~acc~~ accordance with the terms of the Highway Robber's Code of Conduct, demand every one of <u>you lot</u> who is highwaymanning between Lesser Belcham and Eggy Bottom to attend the following MEETING.

<u>NO EXCUSES!</u> or else ➔ ☹

Time: Midnight tonight
Venue: The camp in the woods
Refreshments will be served.

Non attendance will result in immediate striking ~~off the professional register~~ on the head with a
Big Stick

'Where did you get this from, Scratchy?' Lil sat down in the scrubby grass and crossed her legs. 'Come on, then. Come down 'ere you silly thing.' She rooted about in her apron pocket and gently tossed some soggy breadcrumbs onto the floor. Scratchy jumped down and began snapping them up eagerly. 'Where have you been, then? Over by the big woods?'

'*CAAW!*' he said, and carried on jabbing his shiny black beak at the crumbs.

So the highwaymen were having a meeting in the woods, were they? Maybe Lil could go along and spy. They could be dangerous, but Lil figured if they didn't know she was there, she'd be able to get away with it . . . and she might discover a way to stop their activities. It would be tricky to sneak out of the inn at night, but with a bit of luck everyone would go off to bed and leave Lil to her ridiculous list of chores and not notice she was missing. It was just too good an opportunity to miss. Clever Scratchy.

Just as a cunning plan was taking shape, she was interrupted by Arthur Boote.

''Ere, Margery, look who's behind the turnip shed, messing about with that scruffy little crowlet again.'

'*Uuuuuummm,*' added Maude.

'If she's messing about with that disgusting bird instead of doing her chores, I'll tell Ma,' Margery complained.

Lil jumped up and stuffed the notice into her apron pocket, shooing at Scratchy. He flitted over to the hedgerow with a disgruntled squawk.

'What's it got to do with you, Arthur Boote?' she said, coming round the corner of the shed. 'I was looking for a dock leaf actually, thanks to *Margery*.' Lil was less concerned about Margery snitching on her than she was about Arthur snooping into her private space. The turnip shed and the veg patch were Lil's sanctuary.

'That vile bird is vermin, Lil. It's dirty and vicious and Ma says you're not allowed to encourage it. I've a mind to set the cat on it,' Margery snarked.

'It is not vicious or vermin, Margery. It's just a baby crow. Nothing to be scared of, you nitwit.'

'Don't be rude to your sister, Lil. You're not allowed to keep it and them crows spread *the pestilence*.' Arthur always tried to sound posh around Margery. 'And, I might add, in my honest opinion, it is very *strange* for a girl to be hanging about with a crow.'

'Very strange,' said Maude.

'I don't *keep* it. It's a wild animal!' Lil protested. 'It's not

58

my fault Margery's scared of it!' But they weren't listening. Arthur spoke over the top of her.

'What would we expect from the *Queen of Turnips,* anyway, eh? I reckon I might get me a slingshot and 'ave a go at that thing next time I see it. What do you reckon, Margery? Crow stew?'

'You do that, and I'll take a pot shot at you, you great lumbering hummock. You're only trying to show off in front of Margery.'

They were all shouting at once.

Lil started doing her Margery impression: '*Oh Arthur! Save me! I'm terrified of a tiny little baby crow, oh, oh, save me!'*

'WHAT'S GOIN' ON OUT 'ERE?!' Ma emerged from the back door of the inn, looking flustered. 'What are you up to, Lil? I thought it was too quiet upstairs.' She had another grotty tea towel draped over her shoulder and a dark scald patch on the back of her apron where she'd absent-mindedly leaned against the stove.

'Margery pushed me in the nettles and I was finding a dock leaf,' Lil explained.

'And what did you do to Margery to deserve that? That's what I'd like know, young lady.'

'Nothing! I was just giving her the rest of the dirty sheets!'

'And a load of disgusting snotty hankies! I told her I'm not meant to be doing customer laundry! We charge extra for that. But Lil seems to be too stupid to follow simple instructions . . . '

'All right, that's enough, you two! Mr Sprottle is our *only* paying customer at the moment and I'm hoping he might stay for a few more nights, so we should all do our best to make him comfortable. And if that means scrubbing his snotty hankies, I'm afraid we're gonna 'ave to put up with it for now. Lil – you help your sister with that, and stop complaining!'

'She's been playing with that bird again, Mrs Scroggins,' Arthur reported. 'I saw it out the back there.' He turned his self-satisfied grin on Lil.

'Lil? Is that right? I've warned you about that! You ain't got time to be messin' about when there's all this work to be done!'

'I don't see anyone else doing much scrubbing,' muttered Lil.

'Oh you cheeky little . . . ! I'll 'ave that bird and roast it! Besides, it's all them highwaymen's fault,' protested Ma. 'Why can't they keep to their own nasty business and keep outta mine?!' She jabbed her finger at Lil furiously.

'If things 'aven't improved by the end of the week, young lady, I'm seriously considering selling up!' She huffed and snatched the tea towel from her shoulder. 'Margery, come in 'ere and help me in the kitchen. Lil, you can finish off those few bits of washing before dinner.'

'But I've got *loads* to do already!'

'For that cheek, young lady, you can do a full stock take of all the jars in the larder, an' all. And count the biscuits while you're at it. I need to know my assets if we're gonna sell this place. My homemade preserves will prove very popular, I reckon. Tripe and gooseberry jam goes nicely with turnip pie. Anyway, if you don't get ALL your chores sorted by tomorrow morning, I'll 'ave that pesky bird for the pot!'

Lil stood blinking with her mouth open.

'Ha, ha! Roast crow!' sniggered Arthur. 'You know, Mrs Scroggins, I've 'ad pigeon and sparrow, but never crow!'

Lil stomped over to the basket of dirty sheets and upended it into the tub of water. She could hear Arthur, Margery and Maude prattling on about crow pie as they followed Ma back towards the inn. She refused to turn and look at them in case they thought she cared about what they were saying. But the tears were stinging behind her eyes. *I hate them,*

I hate them, I hate them, she fumed. She was still staring into the tub when Ned approached.

'You all right?' he asked carefully. 'What happened to your face?'

'Nothing,' Lil snapped.

Ned could see she had been crying and was covered in stings and dirt, but he didn't want to embarrass her.

'So . . . anything I can do, then? To help?'

'I've just been given a long list of stupid chores to do before morning, and I haven't even finished the first lot.'

'I'll give you a hand, don't worry.'

Lil sighed. 'Thing is, Ned, I've got to go to a meeting tonight.'

'A meeting?'

'It's my only chance to spy on the highwaymen. Look!' She wiped her hands and thrust the piece of paper at him. 'The meeting's at midnight! So I need to get all this lot finished and sneak out.'

'Why are you spying on the highwaymen? They're robbers and thieves – and probably murderers too!'

'Because I want to know what's going on. Maybe I'll be able to work out a way of getting rid of them. Know your enemy and all that.'

'It'll be dangerous! What if you get caught?'

'I'll go in disguise. We can have a rummage in the lost property cupboard later on. Besides, I'm only going to spy on them. If I keep quiet and keep my head down, they won't know I'm there.'

'Well, I can certainly give you some tips on that,' said Ned.

It was true. Lil didn't think her mother, or anyone else at the inn, had even noticed Ned was there. He was just some kind of appendage to Mr Sprottle when his assistance was required, but the rest of the time it was as if he didn't

exist. Ned explained how his entire family prided themselves on being able to blend in with the furniture. A life spent in service meant remaining virtually invisible whilst serving up a twelve course dinner. It was a genuine art form.

'Anyway, my job's not as bad as my brother Roderick's,' Ned explained. 'He works as a portable footrest.'

'Surely not?!' Lil giggled.

'It's true! It's considered a great honour!' Ned insisted.

Laughing, Lil and Ned set to with the list of chores. It was much quicker with two of them working together, and it turned out Ned had a flair for cleaning. Everything was finished with an extra bit of pizzazz, far superior to the usual standard at The Squawking Mackerel.

'So, how come your ma picks on you all the time? What's the deal with that?' Ned asked.

'Firstly, she's *not* my mother,' Lil sighed. 'But I'm supposed to do as she says. My *real* ma died of a fever when I was a baby. I don't remember her.'

'What about your dad?'

'He's aboard a ship. He's an explorer. Well, sort of. He's on a ship, anyway.'

'Oh. Where's he exploring?'

'The *Americas*. Or, around those parts.'

'Will he be back? I mean . . . Do you know when he's expected back?'

A NEW and ACCURATE MAP of THE AMERICAS AND THEREABOUTS etc

THE NORTHERN UNKNOWN (VERY COLD)

CONTINENT of GREENLAND

ICELAND (MORE BEARS LIKELY)

COLD

ICE

NEW NORTH WALES (BEARS)

HUDSON'S BAY

NEW BRITTIAN

CANADA

NEW FRANCE

NEW FOUND LAND

NEW SOUTH WALES

NEW SCOTLAND

NEW YORK

PARTS AS YET UNKNOWN

BEARS

VIRGINIA

CAROLINA

MER DU NORD

CALIFORNIA?

NEW MEXICO (MORE SNAKES)

LA LOUISIANE

SNAKES

FLORIDA

SOMEWHAT STEAMY

BAHAMA ISLANDS

PIRATES

BEARS?

RATHER TOO WARM

GULF DE MEXICO

MEXICO or NEW SPAIN

CARIBBEAN ISLANDS

AMAZ

PACIFICK OCEAN or SOUTH-SEA

BIG SNAKES

SOUTH AMERIKA

'Not exactly. Truth is . . . I was only two when he left, so I don't really remember what *he* looks like either. He left me a note though. It was addressed to "Lil, at The Squawking Mackerel". It said I should be a good girl for *kind* Mrs Scroggins . . . and that he'd come back for me one day.'

'Oh. All right.'

'I mean, obviously I don't know for *sure* that he's gone to the Americas. Or that he's an explorer. But that seems the most likely explanation to me. Everyone else says he was press-ganged, and that he was probably sunk at sea, seein' as nobody's heard from him since. But what do they know? He *could* be an explorer. There's a lot to be explored. It would take a long time to get there and back. To the Americas, I mean.'

It seemed an unlikely story to Ned, but he didn't want to press the issue. The villagers were probably right. Lots of people were press-ganged onto ships that never returned, and criminals were sent away all the time. If that was the case, then Lil's father wouldn't be back at all.

'Yes. I suppose it would take a long time,' Ned agreed.

'Anyway, that's the main reason I'm sticking around here. If I go off gallivanting before he gets back then he won't know where to find me, will he? So, for now I'm stuck here with *kind* Ma Scroggins, dippy Margery and the boring Bootes.'

Ned grimaced.

'There's Scratchy, of course. I'm glad he's here. And now there's you. For a bit at least.'

Ned smiled. 'Yes, I hope we get to stay. Maybe I should waft a draught across Mr Sprottle's feet. That's sure to give him another bout of the sniffles.'

By evening the inn was busy again, but as most of the passengers had again been robbed penniless, they were receiving short shrift from Ma, who told them to trundle back on their way around the Eggy Bottom detour.

A few travellers had escaped the highwaymen, only to come unstuck when they reached the puddle. There were a couple of wagoners who had been transporting cabbages to market. They traded Ma a crate of fresh brassicas in return for a place to put their feet up out of the drizzle for a few hours. Another lucky escapee was a party of aristocrats who were on their way to London in one of the new 'flying' mail coaches. The new-fangled highly-sprung suspension on these coaches was supposed to avoid the usual bumps and jolts of the road, but the contraptions rocked back and forth so much that the passengers frequently arrived feeling too sick to eat anything and retired to their beds immediately – much to Ma's irritation. This particular group reported being accosted

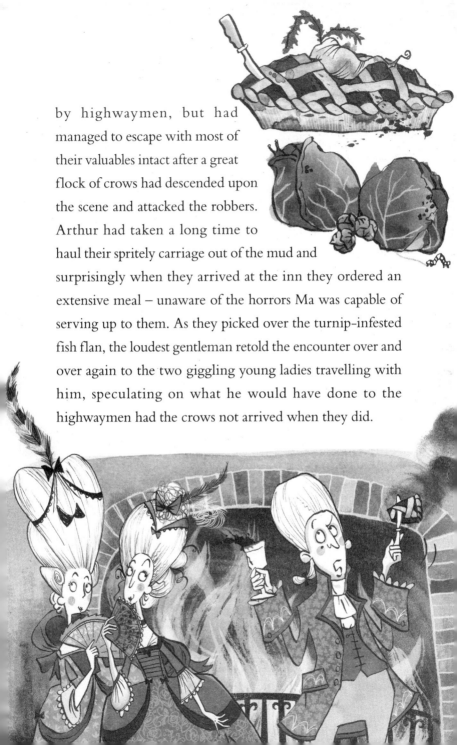

by highwaymen, but had managed to escape with most of their valuables intact after a great flock of crows had descended upon the scene and attacked the robbers. Arthur had taken a long time to haul their spritely carriage out of the mud and surprisingly when they arrived at the inn they ordered an extensive meal – unaware of the horrors Ma was capable of serving up to them. As they picked over the turnip-infested fish flan, the loudest gentleman retold the encounter over and over again to the two giggling young ladies travelling with him, speculating on what he would have done to the highwaymen had the crows not arrived when they did.

Margery hovered around attentively, copying their mannerisms, but the twittering little troupe were far out of her league. Later in the evening, Lil made sure she let Arthur know how much Margery had admired the young gentleman's beauty spot, and Scratchy made off with two sparkly wig ornaments and a snuff box.

As nine o' clock approached, Ned took over washing up the dinner things and Lil snuck off to the lost property cupboard to find a disguise. She unearthed a smallish moth-eaten frock coat, a battered tricornered hat, and a little feathery bejewelled face mask that Scratchy had pinched from the luggage of some society lady during the summer. There had been a craze this year for Venetian masked balls. Lil had seen etchings of the great events in the society newspapers that the wealthier guests left behind: in Venice, elaborately costumed guests were punted along glittering canals in gondolas. Every big house in England had attempted to reenact their own version with varying degrees of success. She supposed a gondola wouldn't look *too* out of place in Eggy Bottom at the moment, what with the puddle – if you ignored the grey clapboard hovels and scrubby farmland either side. She laughed at the idea of the local nobility trying to recreate the canals and gondolas of Venice on their murky, weed-ridden garden ponds. She wondered how many of the local masqueraders had ended up *in* a pond.

Luckily, Sprottle had remained in his room the entire day, with Lil and Ned taking it in turns to trudge up and down the stairs with bowls of greasy soup. Mr Sprottle hadn't eaten much, and after Ned had performed his usual duties and assured him that the contents of the suitcases had all been checked and aired, he'd fallen back to sleep reading *A Brief Treatise on the Arts of Preserving, Pickling, Sousing and Jellying of All Sortes of Fowles for Improvement of the Digestion* from Ma's library of cookery pamphlets.

8

The Masquerade

By a quarter to eleven the inn had settled for the night. The few customers who had the money to stay were tucked up in bed. Margery was putting on a face poultice, and Lil was doing the last of the washing up.

'Don't be too late going to bed, young lady – you gotta be up early in the morning,' said Ma, peering into the kitchen.

'No, Ma, I won't. I'm nearly done, g'night!'

Ma Scroggins paused and frowned suspiciously at Lil for a few moments. 'Have you counted them jars?'

'It'll be done by the time you get up tomorrow,' called Lil cheerily.

Ma paused for a few seconds more, but couldn't find anything else to complain about. 'See that it is, then,' she muttered, and went off to bed, hitching her dressing gown round her middle and lifting the candle stub to light her way up the stairs to her bedroom.

Lil waited about ten minutes after she'd heard Ma's door slam shut and then hurried to the lost property cupboard where she knocked on the door.

'Come in!' called Ned.

Ned had decided to remain in the cupboard, despite Mr Sprottle's upgrade.

Lil giggled. 'Room service!' She produced a shiny apple from her pocket. 'Thanks for helping out today, Ned. You're a proper lifesaver!'

'No trouble. Happy to help,' he grinned back. 'You sure you still want to do this? It could be dangerous.'

'I might not get another chance to spy on them. I'll be fine!'

Ned had helped her to perfect her disguise. Nothing too elaborate so as not to draw attention – just enough to make the right silhouette in the darkness. He had added a couple of extra buttons to the frock coat so that it fit Lil a little better, and had dug out a musty woollen scarf that would obscure Lil's face and bulk out the coat. Ned had removed the feathers and sparkly sequins from the mask and made a small hole in each side. He had pilfered a length of knicker elastic off one of Sprottle's pairs of 'remarkably modern bloomers', and had strung it through the holes to create a tie. The mask was black and hid the top part of Lil's face completely. She would just about pass as a real, if small, highwayman. If you didn't look too closely.

'What are you stuffing into your pockets?' asked Ned.

'Weapons! In case they're armed.' Lil was filling her coat pockets with Ma's leftover pastries. Ammunition for her trusty slingshot.

'I hope you don't need to use that!'

'Don't worry. It's just in case. Now, are you sure you're all right on jar counting duty, while I'm gone?'

'Of course!' Ned replied nervously. 'But, Lil, remember to keep your head down and stay a couple of steps behind everyone else. Don't speak unless you're spoken to, and *always* agree with whatever they're saying.'

'Got it.' Lil gave him a thumbs up.

'Seriously, Lil, don't draw any attention to yourself.'

'I won't!'

She crept along the hallway and gently opened the inner door, closing it behind her with a quiet click. It was chilly so she pulled the makeshift belt of the frock coat a bit tighter round her waist and buttoned the collar up. She carried the hat in her hand as it was too big for her and she didn't want it to blow away. She wound the scarf around her face and tied on the mask, then unlocked the front door and stepped out into the drizzle.

She'd been outside on her own in the dark before. Between the inn and the turnip shed. So this wouldn't be any different. Easy.

Lil wasn't precisely sure where the highwaymen's camp would be but 'the woods' had to mean Clackit Wood, the one up by the lightning oak on the other side of the road, and she knew the way there easily enough. She was sure she'd be able to follow the sound of voices or the glow of a camp fire once she got there. As she hurried along the path to the gate, Lil hoped that Scratchy wouldn't follow her. She had closed up the turnip shed and given him a whole one of Ma's 'Kentish' pasties to contend with, hoping that the thick, dry crust would keep him occupied until the morning. She knew if he followed her and started his usual antics he was sure to draw attention to them both.

The road was deserted. No surprise there. Nobody would be travelling at night. The drizzle lent everything a glum grey pall. There was no moon visible and the stars were veiled in gloom. She expected to hear an owl hooting or a fox yelping, but the surrounding fields seemed empty. A good night for spying.

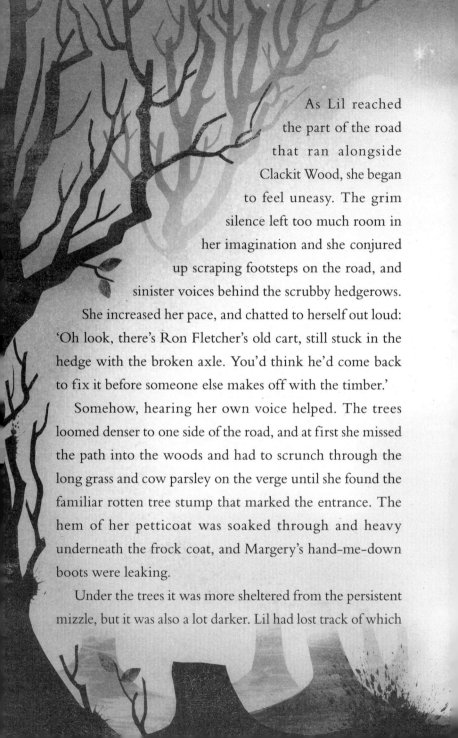

As Lil reached
the part of the road
that ran alongside
Clackit Wood, she began
to feel uneasy. The grim
silence left too much room in
her imagination and she conjured
up scraping footsteps on the road, and
sinister voices behind the scrubby hedgerows.
She increased her pace, and chatted to herself out loud:
'Oh look, there's Ron Fletcher's old cart, still stuck in the
hedge with the broken axle. You'd think he'd come back
to fix it before someone else makes off with the timber.'

Somehow, hearing her own voice helped. The trees
loomed denser to one side of the road, and at first she missed
the path into the woods and had to scrunch through the
long grass and cow parsley on the verge until she found the
familiar rotten tree stump that marked the entrance. The
hem of her petticoat was soaked through and heavy
underneath the frock coat, and Margery's hand-me-down
boots were leaking.

Under the trees it was more sheltered from the persistent
mizzle, but it was also a lot darker. Lil had lost track of which

direction she was aiming for. She became very aware of furtive scurrying sounds in the undergrowth and every so often something bigger crashed away from her, startled by her intrusion into its secret midnight world. She felt an irresistible urge to move faster . . . but she wasn't confident she knew which way to run. 'La, la, la,' she sang to herself. By now, the prospect of being discovered by ruthless highwaymen had become less scary than being eaten by whatever was slinking through the bracken around her. In the centre of the wood the trees were older and bigger and at last it became easier to tell if she was following the right path by looking up at the black silhouettes of the branches, stark against the leaden sky. There was a definite corridor ahead. Heartened, she blustered onwards, ignoring the shambling shapes and creeping shadows either side of her. Eventually she caught the faint scent of wood smoke and heard the very human grumbling of a sizeable group of men. Lil pulled the hat down over her ears and tried to look casual as she strolled towards the gathering.

Highwayman's Code of Conduct.

ALL Highway-persons operating within the bounds and confines of the King's highway, Agree <u>not</u>, by any act, or utterance, to bring the Noble Profession of Highway Robbery into Diskepute.

Strict adherence to the System is required at ALL times regardless of the weather.

Highway-persons found deviating from the SYSTEM will receive a WARNING, Followed by a kick in the shins.

Appropriate headgear must be worn at all times.

No Horse-tampering.   No saddle shining.

No Swashing without a Buckler.

Do Not Leave Equipment Unattended.

No snitching, grassing, blabbing, or Tattling either.

ALL Mugging, Stealing, Burgling, Lifting, Robbing, swiping, poaching, Nicking, Tea-Leafing, pinching, and Thieving is undertaken at your own Risk.

<u>Failure</u> to adhere to the Above mentioned Code of conduct will Result in expulsion From the Guild and a sharp BANG on the Head with a Big Stick. 💀

9

An Exceedingly Boring Meeting

'I Rotten Bob Hatchet declare this parley of the Guild of Highwaymen officially open.'

'Who's the chairman?' asked a beady-eyed little man smoking a noxious pipe.

'I am.'

'So who's taking notes?'

'Swanky Frank du Bonnet 'ere.' Rotten Bob gestured to a flamboyantly dressed fellow with his stripy trousers pulled high up over his substantial belly.

'Who's the vice chairman then?'

'No one. Now sit down and button it! *Item number one*,' Bob announced, 'is that you lot are a useless bunch, and your

substandard thievery has brought this honourable profession into disrepute. And I won't 'ave it.'

The campfire was weak and sputtering as it tried to consume damp wood, belching out thick smoke in response. Rotten Bob stood on a huge tree stump whilst the other highwaymen either sat on logs that had been pulled into a rough circle around the fire, or shuffled about behind them, muttering to each other and sharing a plate of soggy curling sandwiches. Lil stood quietly at the back.

Bob cleared his throat again. 'Now, as you will all be aware, a wise travelling fellow will carry two purses on 'im when undertaking a journey of any considerable distance. One purse for the scoundrels –' he gestured to the highwaymen gathered around him – 'and one purse for 'imself. *Furthermore*, it has long been accepted that your *professional* highwayman –' he gestured to himself – 'will on occasion hold up a coach *twice* – thus relieving the fellow of his second purse and ensuring that he is not allowed to linger under the misconception that he has outwitted a highwayman.'

Several in the front row grunted in agreement and nodded knowingly to each other.

'HOWEVER,' Bob continued, 'it serves no purpose whatsoever to hold up a coach three or more times! It is a

waste of horse-sweat, and it is highly embarrassing to discover that your prey has already been cleaned out by the idiots up the road. It makes us a laughing stock, and *you lot* should be ashamed of yourselves!'

General consternation and objection rumbled through the crowd.

'How are we supposed to know who's been held up before and who hasn't?' asked a young man with a reedy voice, wearing a frilly cravat, and decorative boots.

'What happened to the system?' shouted a bearded fellow from the back.

'With everybody all on the rob at once, the system don't work no more,' observed another.

'Indeed!' interjected Bob. 'And THAT is why I propose . . .'

'Hang on a minute, Bob – I can't write that fast.' Swanky Frank du Bonnet was frantically scribbling at the piece of wrinkled paper perched on his knee.

'You said you knew how to take notes.'

'I do, Bob, but I got stuck on "misconception". Is it two s's or one?'

'I don't know. Just scribble a bit and move on.' Bob turned back to the agitated crowd. 'Now. As I was sayin',

I propose to devise a *timetable* allotting each highway-individual, or gang, an allotted time slot on an allotted patch of road . . . '

'But that's not the way we usually do it, Bob,' warned the young chap with the boots. 'There's nothing in the Code of Conduct about a timetable.'

The disgruntled murmuring swelled.

'Unusual times call for unusual measures,' declared Bob over the growing unrest.

'Oh my almighty Bennett! Hang on, Bob! U-n-u-s-u . . . ' Swanky Frank was struggling to keep up.

'So, who gets to decide who goes when?' questioned the pipe smoker.

'I do,' replied Bob.

'Well, that's not fair! What if I only get cabbage carts and muck spreaders in my allotted time?'

'Look, we can't all do at it at the same time, else NO ONE GETS NUFFINK!' Bob roared.

Lil ducked as a sandwich flew over the crowd and landed with a soggy splat in Swanky Frank's lap.

'Who threw that?'

Two men leaped to their feet as another barged through to the front. They clustered around the tree stump,

remonstrating with wild gestures. One threw his arms up in the air, knocking another on the chin, whose mate took a swing at him. The chinned fellow threw his hat to the ground and stood with his fists up, challenging the first to a fight. Everyone was on their feet now. Lil was shoved in the back as someone was accused of being a 'low-down saddle-shining braggart'. All about her, the highwaymen hurled insults at each other and jostled for a better view of the fight. Lil considered making a sharp exit before things turned really nasty. She was just about to slip back into the woods when all of a sudden the ruckus fell silent. Lil froze.

Bob stood glowering above them all with his arm in the air. In his hand was a huge flintlock pistol. He drew back the hammer with a menacing click.

'Gentlemen, gentlemen!' Bob scoured the crowd with his steely eyes. 'This is a *meeting,* not a bust up.'

The highwaymen nearest to Bob backed away. Others stooped and ducked their heads. Those who had been fighting let go of each other's cravats and shuffled apart, brushing off their trousers and straightening their shirt collars.

Bob slowly released the hammer and tucked the gun back into his belt.

87

'Now that we're all settled, I shall draw up a timetable forthwith,' he continued calmly.

'Hold up, shouldn't we have a vote on it?' It was the beady-eyed pipe smoker again.

Bob glared at him. 'Do you want to be banged on the head with a big stick?'

'No, Bob.'

'Well then, *sit* down and *stop* talking. Now . . . ' He adjusted his waistcoat. '. . . We move on to Any. Other. Business.'

'Hang on a minute, Bob. I'm still writing it down!'

'Writing what down?'

'That Three-Fingered Ted doesn't want to be banged on the head.'

Bob sighed. 'Does anyone want another sandwich while we wait?'

An oversized lumpy-looking fellow spotted Lil and ambled towards her with a friendly rotten-toothed smile. He offered her a sandwich, but when she shook her head, he stood next to her and introduced himself as Monstrous Martin. Lil shook his big mucky hand. She could see the puzzlement growing on his face as he chewed.

'So . . . are you a highwayman, then?' he asked.

'Yes. More or less,' she replied curtly.

He frowned at her for a long time.

'You seem a bit . . . small,' he observed with his mouth full.

'I'm just starting out.'

Lil sank deeper into her scarf and adjusted her mask. She desperately willed him to go away.

Bob raised his voice again over the chatter. 'Have you finished, Frank?'

'Yes, Bob. Thank you, Bob. We have *one* additional item on the agenda, and it is . . . ' Swanky Frank flourished his quill. '. . . Murderous Crows.'

'Murderous Crows?' Bob repeated.

'Yeah! A flock of them ganged up on Martin and stole his lunch today,' an enthusiastic voice rang out from behind

Lil's shoulder. The owner was a garishly dressed man with an elaborately curled moustache. He prodded Monstrous Martin in the back. 'Go on. Tell Bob.'

'They stole me lunch, Bob. Took it right outta me hand.'

Bob stood agape.

Lil began to edge away from Martin and the moustachioed dandy.

'We were holding up one of those new-fangled flying mail coaches,' the moustachioed one continued, 'when the blighters came swooping down and pecked me right on the bonce!'

'The crows *have* been unusually aggressive, Bob,' added Swanky Frank.

'Right creepy, they are,' agreed Martin. 'Always watching. First they look at you through one eye, and then they slowly twist their head and look at you through the other . . . '

'I told you there was something funny going on round 'ere with them crows,' Ted added. 'It's like they're . . . organised.'

'And the stench! It smells like something nasty's died and gone off in that puddle. It's the stench of a grave, that.' It was the bearded one at the back again, but most were muttering in agreement.

Rotten Bob was incredulous. 'Well, now I've heard it all! Grown men scared of a few scrawny birds? What are you?

90

Highwaymen or weeny whiny mice?' He laughed and shook his head. 'Give 'em a swipe and they'll soon clear off. Better still, I'll take a pot shot at 'em. That's what I'll do. Let Blasty Bess 'ere 'ave a go at 'em.' He patted the pistol in his belt affectionately.

Lil scowled at the backs of the highwaymen as they swaggered and bragged about what they would do if they caught any crows stealing their lunch. It was obvious that this Rotten Bob Hatchet was a bossy loudmouth with a high opinion of himself. She hoped the local crows would swoop down and peck *him* on the bonce. The highwaymen were certainly a superstitious lot, but she was surprised at how spooked they were by the crows' territorial behaviour, and the stink from the ditches. Eggy Bottom had always smelled bad, on account of the duck pond burping off sulphurous fumes every so often. Although she had to admit that the pong had got a lot worse since she'd blocked up the drainage ditches. Well, it did no harm to let them believe it was something more sinister, and that gave her an idea. Even though she was only meant to be spying, Lil wondered if she could feed their fears and give them a well-deserved bout of the collywobbles with a spooky story of her own. It might even be enough to send the stinking rascals packing.

Maybe she would stay for a sandwich after all.

'AYE!' The highwaymen shouted suddenly, raising their hats in the air.

All except for Lil, who hadn't been paying attention.

'I said . . . Who's in?' repeated Bob.

Lil blinked and looked around. Everyone was staring at her.

'What about *you*?' Bob narrowed his eyes and fixed her with a suspicious scowl.

'Me?'

'You scared of crows, then?'

'No!' Lil had no idea what he was talking about.

'Then put your money where your mouth is, and put your five shillings in the pot.'

'The what?'

'Whoever strangles the most crows!' explained Martin excitedly. 'Everyone has to put five shillings in the pot then whoever strangles the most crows, or shoots 'em . . . or whatever . . . by the end of the week, he wins the pot!'

'Oh . . . I . . . er . . .'

'You gotta keep the ones you kill though and 'ang em up to be counted. Swanky Frank will keep the tally.'

'Then we can pluck 'em and roast 'em for supper,' Ted added eagerly.

'Oh. I'm . . . No thanks. I'm . . . er . . . not planning on sticking around.' Lil tipped her hat and stuffed her hands into her bulging oversized pockets.

'What you got in yer pockets?' Ted asked curiously.

'Oh nothing. Just some er . . . snacks,' Lil faltered. She hadn't prepared for this.

'Well, let's have a look then.'

Lil pulled out a battered Kentish pasty and slowly opened her hand.

'Looks tasty,' grinned Martin.

'I can assure you it's not.'

'Share and share alike,' chided Ted.

'Well . . . if you really want to, but don't say I didn't warn you.'

Lil pulled the rest of the pastries out of her pockets and offered them out. Martin was first in, followed by the one with the curled moustache. He had reached out for a small pie, but then spotted a rotten sardine head amongst the filling and hesitated. Lil cringed. That was all her ammo gone. 'Mind your teeth,' she added cheerfully.

'So, who are you then?'

It was Rotten Bob. He was standing on his tree trunk with his massive arms folded over his barrel-shaped chest.

She gave her name as Light-Fingered Lucy, and explained that she was just leaving the village on her way to London to learn the distinguished arts of highway robbery and pickpocketing. (She wished she'd had a bit more time to work out what she was going to say.)

'You can't be a highwayman,' observed Bob.

'Why ever not?' Lil exclaimed.

'Cos you're a girl!' he replied.

'I can be a highway*woman*,' Lil replied haughtily.

'There's no such thing,' said Bob, with an air of finality.

'There is too! I come from a long line of villainous thieves.'

'Oh yeah? I've never heard of you.'

'As I said, I'm just starting out.'

It wasn't exactly going to plan. Sensing her cover could be blown at any minute, she steered the conversation in a different direction.

'And I'll give you gentlemen a word of advice. You don't wanna be doin' no robbing and thieving round this neck of the woods. That's for certain.'

'And what would you know about it?' scoffed Bob.

'I told you. I grew up round 'ere.' Lil replied. 'I know this stretch of road very well, and I'm giving it a miss for sure! I wouldn't be hanging round here if I were you. Move on while you can, is what I say.'

This was it. She'd better be able to tell a convincing tale or she'd be done for.

10

The Legend of Ghastly Jack Crowheart

'Haven't you heard of Ghastly Jack Crowheart the Demon Highwayman?' Lil had found a seat on a log and settled herself a little closer to the campfire. She tried to look entirely natural in her oversized hat. 'If he catches you thieving on his patch, he'll feed you to his crows!'

'Never 'eard of 'im!' declared Bob, but more highwaymen had gathered round, sensing a story in the telling. The moustachioed dandy from earlier tried to sit down on a log nearby but his trousers were too tight so he had to stand with one leg up on it instead.

'What's this about crows?'

'Listen.' Lil took a deep breath and leaned in to her audience. 'A long time ago, Ghastly Jack used to prey on travellers along this very stretch of road. He was a murderous, merciless man who would rob his victims and then leave them for dead in a ditch!'

'That's a bit much,' said Monstrous Martin.

'Not entirely unusual though, is it?' asked Three-Fingered Ted. 'Not sure why that makes him a *demon* highwayman?'

'Well, I shall tell you, if you'll be quiet.' Lil shot Ted an angry glance as she continued, '*One* evening, he was goin' about his nasty business, when he came upon this poor old sailor, walking all alone with a pack slung over his shoulder.

He didn't look like he had two brass buttons to rub together, but it had been a quiet day and Jack thought he'd have his wicked fun with the man anyway. Jack lurched out from where he'd been hiding behind that very hedge over there –' Lil pointed towards the road – 'and he growled his usual "Stand and deliver!"'

The highwaymen looked in the direction of the road and then turned back to Lil.

'Well, the sailor stopped and held up his hands. "Spare me, sir! I'm a poor man," he cried. "I've got nothing of value to you."

'"Pah," scoffed Jack. "I'll be the judge of that. Hand over your pack or I'll chop off your thumbs and drown you in

that ditch!" He liked to threaten people, did Jack. Well, the
poor sailor looked at Jack, who was bigger and meaner than
your average highwayman of the time, and he handed over
his meagre belongings. And as it turned out, in the sailor's
pack there was a battered old tin mug, half a tattered old
map and...a tiny heart-shaped ruby!'

The highwaymen were definitely listening now. Lil
continued.

'"Ha! Thought you could trick me, eh?" snorted Ghastly
Jack as he held up the ruby, letting it glint in the moonlight
before tucking it into his top pocket. "Just for that, you lying
old sea-dog, this voyage will be your last!" and Jack grabbed
hold of the sailor by the collar and shook him!

"'Spare me, sir, spare me, please,' cried the sailor. "I can promise you plenty more treasure where that came from. This here is a treasure map. See?" Jack paused mid shake with the sailor hovering over the ditch. "You see," cried the sailor, "I sent the other half home to my dear daughter many years ago. For safe keeping. That little gem is but a fraction of the treasure. If you wait here for me, I promise I'll bring you the other half of the map tomorrow. My only wish is to see my daughter again. You can keep all the treasure. Promise on my life!'"

Lil was stretching her luck with the soppy stuff, but she felt she was on a roll now.

"'Well,' Jack laughed, 'that's a bit rich coming from you.

You've already lied to me once this evening. Do you think me a fool? I've got the ruby and I've got half the map as well! Tell me the name of your daughter and I'll go and fetch the other half myself!"

'The sailor shook his head. "Oh no, sir, I couldn't do that. She'd be terrified if someone like you showed up on her doorstep!"

'"Tell me her name and I'll spare you!" Jack snarled.

'"Never!" cried the sailor.

'And back and forth they went like that until Jack lost his temper.'

Monstrous Martin sat listening with his mouth open. Lil quickly continued while she had their full attention.

'"Right, that's it!" said Jack. And he grabbed the sailor by the scruff of the neck and dragged him into the woods where he tied him to a twisty old tree. A great murder of hungry crows swirled around it and perched on its branches, cawing and eyeing up the sailor, peering at him through one eye...and then the other. "Tell me her name – or I'll feed you to the crows!" Jack roared.'

A branch cracked overhead and the highwaymen glanced about the clearing nervously.

Lil continued: 'All night long the sailor wouldn't talk.

Well, Jack was furious, but he was also greedy and he couldn't let the treasure slip through his fingers. All the next day and all the next night, Jack interrogated the sailor. "Tell me her name," he snarled. But still, the sailor wouldn't crack, even when the crows perched on his head or pecked at his toes! Another day and another night passed, and the sailor grew weak from thirst and hunger. "Tell me her name!" rasped Jack. But the sailor wouldn't reveal the name of his daughter.

'Finally, as the sailor was about to expire and the crows descended to feast upon his bones, he drew in his final breath and uttered a terrible curse upon Ghastly Jack:

'"*You'll never rest until you knows*

And until you rest, you'll walk with the crows!"'

Lil fumbled over that last line. She hadn't really thought of the curse beforehand so had to make it up on the spot, but she said it with theatrical flair so she reckoned she had got away with it.

'Well, that's 'orrible!' declared Monstrous Martin.

'It is,' said Lil, 'and to this *day* the evil ghost of Ghastly Jack Crowheart haunts this *very* stretch of road, seeking new victims. He ties them up to the Crow Tree in the woods, and howls, *"Tell me her name!"* until they die of fright and

the crows peck out their eyes!'

'So hang on a minute,' asked Ted, 'he's got a ruby, but he's still wandering about the woods trying to find out the name of some old sailor's long-lost daughter?'

'He's a restless spirit! He doesn't know the name – so he can't rest, can he?' said Martin excitedly with a mouthful of pie crust. 'Whether 'e likes it or not! He keeps tying people up to that tree to find out. But they don't know the name either, do they? So they end up being fed to the crows, and he carries on creeping about, givin' everyone the heebie-jeebies.'

'Well, I'm not sticking around to be feasted on by no crows,' said the man with the curled moustache.

'I told you I didn't like the look of those rotten crows. I'm shifting off elsewhere,' shuddered another. There were murmurings of agreement from the other highwaymen.

'There's no such thing as a demon highwayman,' interrupted Rotten Bob, who'd remained quiet until now. He swaggered over to the group and stood in front of Lil with his hands on his hips and his jacket tucked behind Blasty Bess. 'I reckon you're pulling our leg! Trying to swipe this patch all for yourself, are you?'

'I'm only telling you what I know,' said Lil. 'Make of it

what you will, but personally, I wouldn't stick around here and take the risk.'

'What's 'e look like then, this Ghastly Jack?' asked Bob.

'They say he's massive – over six-and-a-half foot tall and wide as a door, with a deathly white face. He's got glowing red eyes, and he stinks of the grave!'

'Well, you wouldn't smell 'im coming with Bob around!' sniggered Ted nervously.

'You may laugh,' Lil warned, 'but they say in these parts, that when he's on the prowl you can hear the bloodcurdling cries of his victims as the crows peck out their eyes!'

Then, right on cue, a streak of black feathers shot out of the trees and swooped over their heads, dumping a beakful of twigs and spiders and beetles. Scratchy plunged down into the undergrowth with a blood chilling *'CAAAAAAW!'*

11

Beetle Blast

The highwaymen leaped to their feet, brushing creepy crawlies out of their hair. They flapped at their collars, rattled their hats and shook out their trouser legs. The camp was in uproar.

'That's it. I'm off!' shuddered the man with the overly decorative boots. 'I might take my five shillings back, if you don't mind, Bob?'

'Shall I cross you off the timetable then?' Bob jeered. 'Go on, then. Cowards, the lot of ya! And good riddance.'

Despite the jeers, several of the highwaymen gave their excuses and left. Bob continued to poke fun at them as they went.

'Demon highwayman? Pah! Once all the lily-livered bags of wind have scuttled off, there'll be richer pickings for me,' he bragged, 'and all the more loot for my fine colleagues 'ere. Eh, lads?' Those of Bob's more immediate circle who had remained in the camp looked reluctant, but Bob slapped them jovially on the back as he strutted around them, telling them of the splendid opportunities they would enjoy if they stuck with him.

Lil had been delighted at Scratchy's timely intervention with the beetles, but to her dismay she saw that he had returned to the clearing and was now hopping about the campfire gobbling sandwich crumbs, and hunting down the straggling beetles and spiders he had dropped. She tried not to look at him. Without his tail feathers he was vulnerable. He couldn't fly properly, so he really needed to make himself scarce in case anyone fancied taking a pot shot at him.

'Get away, you rotten thing!' One of the highwaymen kicked out viciously at Scratchy as he gathered up his belongings.

'Oi!' snapped Lil. 'Don't do that!'

'Why not?' growled Rotten Bob, who was back at his perch on the tree stump.

Lil turned towards him and gasped in horror.

'Keep still, you scrawny bag of feathers...' Bob muttered as he aimed Blasty Bess's long soot-stained barrel at Scratchy. He pulled back the heavy hammer. *Click.*

'Don't!' Lil yelped, darting between Scratchy and the gun.

'What's it to you?' Bob asked, surprised.

'Nothing!' Lil replied. She kicked the leaf mulch at Scratchy. 'Go on, get away, you mucky thing!'

Scratchy scooted himself up onto a nearby log and stood looking at her quizzically.

'I think it likes you,' snorted Bob.

'Look! It's got no tail!' remarked Swanky Frank. 'Strangle it!'

'It must be half-witted, like she is! Quick, kill it!' urged Ted.

They all laughed.

'If you reckon you're a highwaywoman – prove it!' Bob goaded her. 'Why don't *you* kill it.'

Scratchy hopped back and forth questioningly. It broke Lil's heart. She wanted to scoop him up and carry him back safely to the turnip shed. Instead, she scooped up a hard chunk of discarded pastry and took the slingshot out of her pocket.

'Go on. Kill it,' sneered Bob.

Lil felt the colour drain from her cheeks. They were all watching her. She loaded her slingshot and pulled back the elastic. *Go away, Scratchy. Please.* But Scratchy just stood there with his head cocked to one side, staring at her. She released the missile. It hit the log below him with a vicious *thwack*. He screeched and flapped off into the brambles, squawking in confusion. She cringed as she heard him scrambling deeper into the undergrowth.

Lil felt terrible.

Bob laughed at her.

'You're not a *highwaywoman* in training. I reckon you're just a scrappy little crowlet who's too big for her boots.'

Lil scowled at him defiantly.

'I bet you couldn't even steal the eggs from a sparrow's nest.'

'Why would I want to do that?'

'Why wouldn't you?'

'That's stupid,' Lil threw back at him.

But it made no difference. Bob was in full flow and his gang was scrambling to impress him, sniggering and snorting. Lil turned to walk away.

'Bet you're scared of spiders,' Ted spluttered.

'I am not!' Lil stooped and grabbed one of the creepy crawlies Scratchy had dropped, and held it out in her hand. 'Look!'

'Pull the legs off it then!'

Lil tossed the spider away, hoping it would land somewhere safe.

'Ah, look, she won't do it! She's scared of spiders!' he cackled.

'Go on, pick up that worm and chuck it in the fire!' sniggered Martin.

'No!' Lil spun away from them. What could she do? There was no way she was going to do something so unspeakably

cruel just to satisfy the likes of them. Lil fumed as she stormed from the clearing.

'You'll never be a highwayman,' Rotten Bob called after her, 'because you're too pathetic and too *small*.'

Seething, Lil worked through her options as she stomped back through the woods towards the road. The highwaymen's raucous laughter followed her.

Poor Scratchy. She'd never been mean to him like that before. Would he ever forgive her? What if he went away and never came back? The thought of never seeing him again crushed her heart. It was all Rotten Bob's fault. She'd had no choice! And it was all for nothing *anyway* if that big bully carried on robbing and looting as he pleased. In fact, she'd probably done him a favour by scaring his rivals off. It was so unfair!

There was no way she was going to let that arrogant stinker have the last laugh. She swore she'd have her revenge on him. Somehow.

12

Cauliflower Brains and Nasty Names

By the time Lil got back to the inn, Ned had done a full stock take of the larder, wiping clean the dirty lids and labels, and sorting the spoiled jars into a wheelbarrow. He had tidied up the kitchen too. Several of the jars at the back of the shelves had holes pecked in the lids, and the contents were now sprouting colourful mould. He suggested hiding those under the turnips in case anyone else saw them and Scratchy got in trouble. The further back on the shelves he'd gone, the more gross it had got. 'Your mother should rotate them so that the older jars are at the front, that way they get used up first.'

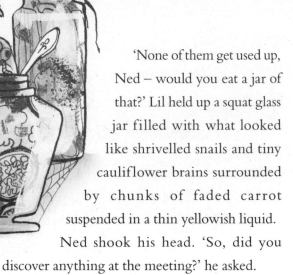

'None of them get used up, Ned – would you eat a jar of that?' Lil held up a squat glass jar filled with what looked like shrivelled snails and tiny cauliflower brains surrounded by chunks of faded carrot suspended in a thin yellowish liquid.

Ned shook his head. 'So, did you discover anything at the meeting?' he asked.

'Yes! They're scared of crows. At least, *some* of them are.'

Ned frowned. 'What do you mean?'

Lil relayed what she had overheard at the camp about the crow attack, and how superstitious some of the highwaymen had been. 'They aren't too happy about the stink coming from the ditches either. They're definitely spooked by it.'

'Well, that's something, I guess, and at least you got away without being noticed.'

'Er . . . that bit didn't *exactly* go to plan . . .'

'Lil! What happened?'

'They're not as ruthless as everyone makes out. Smelly, mainly, very stupid, and terrible taste in clothes . . . but . . .'

'What happened? What did you do?'

'There was a misunderstanding...and then I had to tell them a story, and then some of them ran away. But Rotten Bob (he's the worst) got all suspicious and started on me, and now Scratchy's gone and I don't know if he'll come back.'

'Oh no, Lil. Why were you telling them a story? I thought you said you were going to keep your head down!'

'I did! But they wanted me to go round killing crows for some silly game, and they wanted me to pay them five shillings for the privilege! Then they started questioning me, and I had to make up a story about being a highwaywoman in training, and then I made up this story about a demon highwayman, to scare them off and it worked...at first.'

'How did Scratchy get involved?'

'He must have escaped from the turnip shed and followed me. He turned up squawking at the end of the story and dumped a load of creepy crawlies on the highwaymen. It was great! He really scared them. But then he kind of hung around, picking at the pastry crumbs left over from when Monstrous Martin ate my ammo, and that's when it all went wrong.'

Ned looked confused.

'Rotten Bob tried to shoot him,' Lil continued, 'so I had to intervene. And then that idiot wanted *me* to prove I was a real highwaywoman by taking a shot at Scratchy *myself*! I shot a bit of pastry at him... and missed on purpose! But I don't think Scratchy understood. Ned, what if he never comes back?'

Lil's eyes glistened and she dropped her head into her hands.

'I'm sure he will,' said Ned gently. 'He's probably just a bit confused. We can look for Scratchy in the morning. Maybe it's best to leave this Rotten Bob alone. He sounds horrible!'

'No way! I'm not letting him win. Rotten Bob is the key to this mess. If I get rid of him, all the others will follow and things will go back to normal. Besides, I've sworn revenge.'

'Lil, just leave it! You'll make things worse. Let's try to unblock the ditch instead, then maybe Rotten Bob will move on anyway if the coaching traffic returns to normal.'

Lil was tired. Maybe Ned was right. What could she do to get rid of a nasty brute like Bob anyway? Maybe she should just concentrate on the drains. Mud and drizzle, that's all she was good for.

'I don't know,' she said as she fought back a yawn. 'I can't decide what to do right now.'

'Come on,' said Ned, 'we'd better get to bed, it's nearly light!'

Lil and Ned agreed they should at least try to catch a few hours' sleep before everyone resurfaced in the morning. By the time Lil climbed the stairs to her room in the attic and hid away her highwayman's disguise, she could barely keep her eyes open. She lay her head on her pillow and tried to sleep, but in the cold creaking predawn light, her mind wouldn't switch off.

13

Scratchy Alone

Scratchy had spent the night hunched in the depths of a bramble bush. He had listened carefully to all the night creatures scrabbling and searching. Busy. There would be teeth and claws out too. Stalking. Looking for a crow-sized snack like him. It wasn't safe for a young crow to be out of the roost, alone, at night. Especially a crow who couldn't fly very well.

He had wanted to flap up to join the big crows in the roost, but he couldn't reach the branches of the great lightning tree. So he had crept into the undergrowth and stayed frozen still, watchful and awake until the sky turned brighter grey and the other birds began their morning banter.

He had thought he was helping. He had scraped through the gap in the shed and followed the little one along the big track, deep into the plenty-trees. Her sound had been different tonight. He'd had to be quiet. Sneaking so she wouldn't hear him or see him and send him back. Along the way, he had hunted out the scurriers and slinkers that lived in the tree trunks. He had pounced on the crawly crackle-shells and prickly wrigglers, and caught a big leggy creeper in his beak. But he had not eaten them. Instead he had saved them up.

When he'd caught up with her she had been with the Nasty Faces. They were perched around a big orange scorcher, going *chatter chatter chatter*, and the little one went *crar rar raaaah* for a long time, and then she had to *CAAAW* and shout at them.

He had dropped the wrigglers and crawlers on the Nasty Faces then. They had leaped and jumped and hopped and flapped. And when they flapped and slapped, it made the wrigglers bite and sting more! Ha! That had made lots of the Nasty Faces go away – though not that big stinker.

He had thought the little one would be pleased with him. But instead she had thrown something hard at him, and he had been afraid. He had followed her back through the plenty-trees then, but had kept his distance. Was she mad at him? She had locked him in the shed earlier that night too. Maybe she didn't want to play with him any more?

14

Ditch Disaster

The next morning when Lil and Ned went to check if Scratchy had found his way back to the turnip shed, Lil hoped with all her heart to find him perched grumpily on the turnip shovel. But there was no disgruntled *CAAW* to greet her as she pushed open the door.

He wasn't there.

'I'm sorry, Lil,' Ned said quietly.

Lil felt tears throb behind her eyes again. She felt sick. A cold creeping panic threatened to overwhelm her. She looked away from Ned's kind face, and swallowed.

'I'm going to take these scraps down to the ditch like I usually do. No point in making Ma or any of the others

suspicious,' she sighed. 'But I'll see if I can find out what's causing the blockage while I'm there.'

Lil already knew what was causing the blockage. Three months' worth of stale dumplings and rancid turnip flan. But she couldn't tell Ned that. She wrenched the old turnip shovel from its place in the shed and rattled about until she found a long pointed stick. It was an old broom handle. 'I'll try to get this done before Arthur and Maude head out to the puddle for carriage-hauling duties,' she continued, ashamed of her dishonesty with her friend.

'Good luck,' said Ned. He was wanted indoors to ferry Mr Sprottle's breakfast up the stairs. Mr Sprottle had decided one more day of complete bed rest should see him back to good health, and Ma had been only too pleased to oblige. 'And don't worry, I'm sure Scratchy will turn up. He's probably out hunting for worms in this weather.'

'Hopefully,' Lil replied, as she loaded the shovel and stick into her wonky wheelbarrow and pushed it out of the back gate of the yard.

It was a heavy, foggy morning, with an icy blanket of mist smothering the fields and making the familiar track disappear ahead of her. As quietly as she could, pushing a wobbly clanking wheelbarrow, she trudged towards the

emptiness. She was still dazed from the previous night's adventure.

When she reached the ditch, the world was wrapped in chilly damp silence. Only her footsteps squeaked in the wet grass. She jumped down into the boggy hollow where the top of the culvert was just visible above the brown sludge, and peered helplessly at the mouldering pile she had dumped at the mouth of the drain. On the other side of the road, the water brimmed over the banks of the drainage channel and flooded the neighbouring field. The drowning hedgerow on that side looked like twiggy survivors swept adrift in a sea of ditchwater. It stank. She took the long stick and prodded the top layer of the self-cemented dumpling dam. Perhaps she could break it up by levering bits off? Carefully, she climbed on top of the crumbling culvert and started probing for a good gap to wedge the stick in. At first there was no budging the pile, but after a few attempts she managed to dislodge a small lump. She tried again in the same spot, bending the stick to its limit to shift the next solid lump.

Then the stick snapped and Lil stuck her foot on the bank in an effort to save herself from falling in. Her foot sank through cold slime up to her knee.

It was no good, she would have to shovel some of the silt away first.

She wedged herself across the drain with one foot on either bank, her soggy petticoats flapping against her legs, and crunched the turnip shovel into the sludge. She flicked a load up onto the bank. The water drained from the little pile of silt to reveal the fluted edge of a pie crust. It was still intact despite being submerged for at least a week. No wonder no one ate Ma's pastries. As fast as Lil shovelled, more sludge seeped into the ditch to fill the culvert again. It was like bailing out a sinking ship. But Lil shovelled on.

The more she shovelled, the wetter and muddier she got. As the sun rose and the mist began to lift, she realised that she was being watched.

It was Mirabelle, Arthur's cow. As Lil glanced at her, Mirabelle took it as an invitation, and plodded towards where Lil stood straddling the ditch.

'No, no, no . . . stop, Mirabelle!' Lil didn't want to draw more attention to what she was doing. 'No, Mirabelle . . . stay away,' she warned gently.

But Mirabelle trundled over to Lil, her head nodding hopefully. 'Mooooo?' she enquired.

'Shhhh. Good girl. I'm busy right now. I'll give you a treat later. Go on . . . go back now.'

But Mirabelle stood there expectantly, bobbing her head and swishing her tail. Lil scrambled further down the ditch, out of the line of sight from the inn. The last thing she needed was an audience.

'Urrgh!' She put her foot through something very soft, then she felt the bank give way under her and she slid down in an avalanche of pebbles and weeds to land with a splash, waist deep in stinking ditchwater. Gasping for breath, Lil clambered up the bank, grabbing clumps of couch grass to haul herself up the slippery slope, and crawled into Mirabelle's field. So much for keeping a low profile. She sat shivering in the mud for a few moments, staring ahead of her, when suddenly an evil-looking figure caught her eye. Lil felt a chill of panic, then realised she was staring at a scarecrow. She must be tired. Mirabelle puffed gently and nuzzled Lil's hair.

Where was Scratchy? The scarecrows never frightened him.

It was hopeless. She'd never be able to clear the drains. The road was well and truly flooded, and Rotten Bob and his crew were here to stay.

Sitting in the cold wet mud, Lil looked around. Bleak brown furrows surrounded her. The fields had been ploughed and planted recently, but very few green shoots braved the drizzle and poked their heads above the dark clods of soil. Three scarecrows stood stark against the brightening grey sky, stick arms tilted at abrupt angles as if shouting silent shrieks of alarm. Dressed in old hats and mouldering jerkins, the crows ignored them, but Lil found them to be uncannily eerie, frightening even, as they loomed out of the mist. Like ghostly figures.

Like the ghostly figure of a demon highwayman.

That was it! What if she dressed up as Ghastly Jack Crowheart? Not to scare crows, but to scare the highwaymen?

Lil scrambled out of the mud and brushed off her skirt as best she could. It was mid-morning and the travellers would be starting along the road towards the puddle. Arthur and Maude might already be there. She didn't want them to see her covered in muck, but there was no helping it. She retrieved the broken stick from the bottom of the ditch and tossed it into the wheelbarrow. She had to strain to pull it out of the muck where it had begun to sink, but with an almighty heave she got it moving and pushed it up out of the field and back along the track.

There they were. The bloomin' Bootes. Maude was standing next to the sign slowly twisting her hair and tutting as Arthur inspected the wheels of a wagon wedged up to its axles in the mud. There was something odd in the middle of Arthur's chin. It looked suspiciously like a drawn-on beauty spot. Lil tried not to catch his eye as she shuffled along with the wheelbarrow. The fog had finally lifted, but now the puddle had begun to warm up in the sun, it smelled as if something really had died in there.

'Look who it is, eh? It's the Queen of Turnips, herself,' said Arthur. 'Your ma was looking for you.'

'Arthur, you have a customer,' Lil replied politely, trying not to stare at his chin.

'Yes I'm aware of that, Miss Smartyknickers. Don't get your bloomers in a twist. What happened to you? And leave Mirabelle alone, she's got work to do.'

Mirabelle had followed Lil up from the ditch. Arthur tried to drag the cow away but she wouldn't budge. He slapped her on the haunches and went round the back to give her a push instead. Mirabelle lifted her tail and farted, right in Arthur's podgy face. Maude smirked. Even the wagoner started chuckling.

'Come on, lad,' the man sniggered, 'let's get this cart hauled out. There's a penny in it for your trouble.'

Arthur shot Lil a thunderous look. But she was already skipping off up the lane with the wheelbarrow. She had a plan.

15

Pickle Plans

'Where have you been, young lady?' Ma demanded, as soon as Lil opened the back door of the inn. 'Look at the state of you!'

'Dumping out the rubbish,' Lil replied, trying to scuttle past Ma and out of the kitchen before she got dragged into some new chore. She needed to find Ned.

'Oh no, you don't.' Ma intercepted her and slammed the kitchen door shut. 'I wanna word with you.'

Lil sighed loudly and slumped to attention.

'I don't know what you think you're up to, young lady, sneaking about the place at all hours. I heard you last night! Chatting away with that clothes-rack boy. There's no time

for fraternising with
the customers and their
staff. It's crunch time for
this family! Now, I know
you're not my own, but I'd like
to think I've brought you up
as if you were. And I'm happy
to do it, I'm a community-minded
woman and all that. But you've got to
pull your weight. If we can't turn a profit
these next couple of nights, this 'ere coaching inn will
be up for sale! Now, as I've said before, I'm willing to take
you with me, Lil. I wouldn't dream of sending you off to
one of them workhouses or orphanages. But know this: I
expect you to take on greater responsibility in the running
of this business. It's an opportunity, young lady. Anyone
would be grateful for the kindness and care you've
'ad off me!'

'Yes, Ma. Thank you, Ma. Save the inn.' Lil nodded.
*That's exactly what I'm trying to do if only you'd let me get on with
it*, she thought.

'I'd hoped things were looking up, I really had, but I
can't make enough money if them highwaymen have robbed

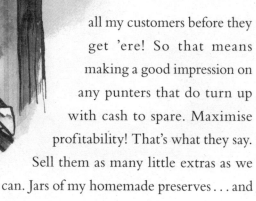

all my customers before they get 'ere! So that means making a good impression on any punters that do turn up with cash to spare. Maximise profitability! That's what they say. Sell them as many little extras as we can. Jars of my homemade preserves... and homemade picnic hampers of my delicious pastry creations to take with them on their journey. I've put a lot of effort into this place, Lil, and I expect you to do the same...'

As Ma droned on, Lil edged towards the door.

'...I need you to make a pickle display in the front lounge window, and a big sign... before the lunchtime crowd arrives... oh, and you can take that old mattress from the first floor annexe out the back and give it a good beating. Nothing but mud and dirt tramped through 'ere these days. I'll 'ave to make a new rule I reckon. No boots on in bed! Filthy habits, these people...'

'Yes, Ma. On it now!' She scuttled out of the room, closed the door, and sprinted up the stairs two at a time. Selling pickles wasn't going to turn around the fortunes of The Squawking Mackerel. But if Lil's plan worked, then

Ghastly Jack Crowheart, the
Demon Highwayman, might.

As she scooted past Mr Sprottle's
room and skidded to a halt, Ned opened the
door a crack and peered out, his finger over his lips.
'Shhhh. He's nodding off,' he mouthed silently, and
retreated back into the room, clicking the door closed
quietly behind him.

Lil was impatient. She had a brilliant plan. She knew it
could work, but she needed Ned's expertise in the sewing
department. She crept along the creaking landing to the first
floor annexe room. The low wooden door emitted a waft
of sweaty leather and cabbages as she opened it. What a
mess. She dragged the rough woollen blankets off the bed

and kicked them into a pile in the corner. It was a small room with just enough space for a pallet bed and a battered tin washbasin perched on an old barrel. She cranked open the warped wooden window frame. 'That's better,' she sighed, as the chilly air rushed in.

With the benefit of daylight, she had a proper look around the room. The cabbage cart bloke had stayed in here. Nothing of interest left behind. It did look like he'd gone to bed with his boots on though. Lil didn't blame him. There were rats behind the skirting boards up here that might nibble your toes. She had rolled up the threadbare sheet and started to haul the straw mattress off the bedframe, when there was a quiet knock at the door behind her.

'Sleeping like a baby,' Ned grinned.

Lil dropped the mattress. 'Ned! I've got a plan!' she whispered urgently.

'Did you unblock the drains?'

'No.' Lil waved her hand to dismiss the idea. 'I'm gonna dress up like Ghastly Jack Crowheart...you know, from my story...and scare

Rotten Bob Hatchet out of his wits!'

Ned didn't answer.

'Listen, I've worked it all out. I'll dress up like Ghastly Jack, and lurk about the side of the road opposite the woods. Then, when Bob and his cronies come by from their day of robbing our customers, I'll pop out of the hedge and give 'em a right fright. It'll have to be tonight though, cos Ma is *this* close to selling the inn. And I'll need your help, Ned!'

'But . . . Lil?'

'It'll be fine! We can have another rummage in the lost property cupboard, you know, to make me a costume. Will you help me?' She looked at him pleadingly.

'Yes, of course! But, Lil . . . I'm not sure I can make you look like a six-foot-tall ghoul! How will you scare them? What if they think you're just another highwayman trying to muscle in on their patch?'

'Don't worry. I've thought of that. A bit of theatrics, and a few cleverly placed rumours should do it. The ghostly figure of Ghastly Jack Crowheart has been haunting the road . . . howling "Tell me her naaaaaaame . . . !"'

'Lil!'

'We can start spreading rumours about ghostly sightings around the inn! Gossip spreads quicker than butter in Eggy

137

Bottom so the highwaymen are bound to get wind of something spooky going on. Then I can go and deliver the final blow!'

'You'll get in big trouble.'

'It's just a story. You can't get in trouble for telling a story.'

'You can, Lil. Especially if it's not true. And what if you get caught out there in the hedge?'

'Seriously, Ned, Bob and his crew are really daft. They're more gullible than Arthur! I can't wait to see the look on Rotten Bob's face!'

They dragged the mattress down the stairs together, *thump . . . thump . . . thump.* Ned cringed at the noise, but nothing stirred in Sprottle's room.

'I'll help you, Lil, but I'm worried you'll just end up in worse trouble. Things could turn nasty! Didn't you say Bob had a pistol?'

'Yeah, "Blasty Bess", he calls it. What an idiot. I'm going to give him such a good scare, though.' Lil looked down the hallway. Good, Ma was still in the kitchen. 'Come on, let's take this out the front door and drag it round to the stables. I don't want to bump into Ma again after the earful she just gave me.'

16

Arthur Boote's Beauty Spot

By the afternoon, there was a queue of travellers at the puddle because Arthur and Mirabelle couldn't haul the carriages out fast enough. Maude was no help, of course. Her job was to tell people about the nice, comfortable inn within walking distance – *not* to shift carts. She ignored Arthur's struggles as she stood twisting her hair and repeating her lines, 'Oh, dear sirs. There is a glimmer of hope for ye. For as luck would 'ave it, up that hill is an inn where an extraordinary welcome awaits ye. And yer can get yer 'orses fixed up there too.'

A crowd of miserable, muck-splattered travellers gathered at the inn, each hoping to be greeted with the promised

'extraordinary welcome', only to find themselves arguing with Ma over a half-stale slice of yesterday's turnip tart. Desperate for a place to stay and a warm meal, some of the posher customers had become *unreasonably quarrelsome*, in Ma's opinion. After a long day suffering the indignities and perils of the highway, several had offered 'promissory notes', in return for their board and lodgings. Ma preferred hard cash over a promise, and was having none of it. Overstretched tempers snapped, and the pickles were not selling either.

Lil couldn't wait for everyone to go to bed. Margery had been particularly bad-tempered that evening, Maude was unbearable as usual, and Arthur was sulking because Margery had pointed out that he had a strange little spot of boot polish stuck on his chin. She had told him to wipe it off in case he put people off their food. Lil had done her best to insert the ghostly goings-on of the demon highwayman into every conversation, but in the end she had just told Maude about it, and watched as she and Margery spread the gossip for her. It was the one thing they were both good at.

At last, the inn shut up for the night, and Lil went to scavenge something to eat from the kitchen of horrors, before calling on Ned in the cupboard.

Mr Sprottle had woken up feeling no better that evening, and Ma had once again made a great fuss of sending him his supper in bed. Ned didn't think Ma's soup was helping... and he was certain that her medicinal tea was making things worse. But Mr Sprottle was a great believer in folk remedies, and had been persuaded by Ma to try a traditional tonic to 'clear him out' before he went to sleep that evening. 'I shall

be emptying his chamber pot all night, I'm sure,' Ned explained gloomily. However, Mr Sprottle's continued illness meant Ned had had time to work on Lil's demon highwayman outfit. Raiding the suitcases, he had adjusted the elastic on a pair of navy blue bloomers so that Lil could wear them tucked into her stockings as breeches. He'd lent her his own waistcoat and had dug out some fancy-looking brocade to make a cravat. He'd also straightened out the tricornered hat, and added an ostrich feather as a flourish.

'The look we *aspire to* on this particular occasion is *gaudy* and *distasteful*,' he declared in his best *Mr-Sprottle-presenting-a-new-underwear-design* voice.

'I think you've captured it splendidly,' said Lil. 'And while we're at it, I'm going to need a different pair of boots. Those old ones of Margery's leak, so I'll see if I can dig out something a bit fancier from this lot.' She gestured to the lost property and bric-a-brac stacked at the back of the cupboard.

'Who leaves their boots behind?'

'You'd be surprised what people leave behind! I doubt we'll find a good pair of riding boots, but there might be something useful lurking at the back of the cupboard.'

As it turned out, there were several odd shoes and boots to choose from. Lil ended up with two left boots – one tall

and dark brown with the sole flapping off, and the other a scuffed black knee-high number with a wobbly heel. They looked much more grown up than her own boots and would pass as a pair in the dark.

'How does it happen?' Ned asked. 'Losing your boots, I mean. I see it when I'm travelling with Mr Sprottle. A random shoe on a wall or by the side of the road. How do you lose a shoe and not notice? Sometimes there's even a pair! How did *that* happen? Was the person snatched out of their boots by a bear?'

'It's a puzzle,' Lil agreed, 'but as far as The Squawking Mackerel is concerned, I reckon it's because they can't wait to get out of here quick enough. Someone left a servant behind once. An elderly chap. He was just making his way to the carriage when it shot off round the corner!'

It was awkward walking in two left boots, but as they were far too big for her anyway, Lil figured she could manage with some extra stockings stuffed inside. She tied her hair back in a tight braid, and loaded up the frock coat with

144

her slingshot and dumplings. As a final precaution she tucked the iron poker from the fireplace into her sash. It would look like a sword in the dark.

'You look . . . disreputable,' said Ned.

'Good! Let's hope the highwaymen think so too!'

'You'll have to try to look . . . bigger. Swagger about a bit.'

'I've got no choice with two left feet,' she giggled. 'But I don't want them to get too good a look at me. I want to be more of an apparition, lurking in the shadows.'

'Lurking would be safer,' Ned agreed. 'Maybe you need something to give your face a more ghostly look?'

'Someone left their make-up purse behind last summer. I had to hide it from Margery, or she'd have had the lot. There might be something in there we can use.' Lil pointed to a shelf behind the door with assorted baggage and personal effects. 'It's underneath that night cap.'

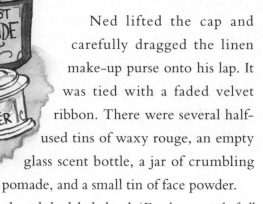

Ned lifted the cap and carefully dragged the linen make-up purse onto his lap. It was tied with a faded velvet ribbon. There were several half-used tins of waxy rouge, an empty glass scent bottle, a jar of crumbling pomade, and a small tin of face powder.

Ned read the label aloud: '*For the removal of all deformities; Ringworm, Scurf, Pimples and pits of the Smallpox. Restores the skin to a persistent and extreme whiteness.*'

'I might just use a bit of flour instead,' said Lil. 'I'll grab a handful on my way out.'

'Yeah. We don't want to give you a permanent ghost face.'

'I wish Scratchy was around. He could have been my ghostly crow sidekick.'

'I'm not sure you could have got him to stay still long enough.' Ned laughed.

'No. You're probably right.'

Lil was nervous, but she didn't want to make Ned any more anxious than he already was. She was just going to wait by the road, make a ghostly appearance, mumble some spooky lines and then slip back into the hedge.

'I'm going out the back way this time, through the kitchen.'

'All right. I'll probably still be up when you get back anyway. Be careful, Lil!'

'I will.' She smiled. 'Thanks for helping out again.'

Ned smiled back.

Lil hobbled quietly through the lounge past the fireplace, scooping a handful of ash from the grate as she went. She rubbed it down the front of the frock coat, then crept into the kitchen to find the heavy jar of flour Ma used for her pastry. She carefully sprinkled a handful over her hat and coat, and patted the rest onto her cheeks.

Opening the back door as quietly as she could, she poked her head out into the yard. It was windy tonight and she could hear the inn sign squeaking back and forth on its hinges. The turnip shed was shuttered just as she had left it earlier that evening, and the day's washing was still flapping on the line where Margery had forgotten to take it in. At least it wasn't raining.

17

Bickering bushwhackers

'Y̲ou were supposed to take over *after* the Scarlet Pomegranate had his turn, not before, *and* you did two stick-ups in a row, cos I was further round the bend and I got two coaches that 'ad already been done, one after the other!' Three-Fingered Ted was clearly not happy with the robbery timetabling arrangements.

'No! That was only cos one coach was faster than the other and overtook the carts that was going along at a slower pace and caught up with the first one.' Swanky Frank protested his innocence, but Ted was convinced he was being swindled.

'Well, I bagged three whole crows today!' bragged Monstrous Martin, as he swigged from his ale pouch.

'One of them was *mine*!' complained Ted. 'I had it cornered until you came lumbering up and set off the trap early!'

Scratchy watched the Nasty Faces from the depths of a prickly gorse bush.

These were the ones who had been mean to the little one, and made her throw things at him. They thumped through the scrubby woods, and everyone was scared of them.

The big crows had shouted at them again today, but they had been more wary this time. That big stinker had the

stick-that-went-bang, and the elder crows thought it was dangerous – lethal, even. Scratchy wasn't sure. But one crow couldn't mob them on his own. Especially not at night.

He was tired of being outside the roost. It was much better in the turnip shed with the little one bringing him scraps to eat. He blinked, hopped off his branch and shuffled into some nettles. He probed under a log with his beak and snaffled a squiggly wriggler that had thought it was tucked up safe for the night. He would go back to the shed and find the little one. She would know what to do.

That meant navigating the immediate dangers of the dark. He could fly short distances from low bush to fence post, but without tail feathers he could not land accurately or quietly. Stealth was key at night. It was a risk to move through the undergrowth as he did, but it was the only way to reach the little one and the safety of the shed. He hopped and crept, hid and watched. Ever wary of a

sudden pounce from the
hedgerow or being silently
snatched by the screechers
above, he listened for the
crunching of leaves or the breath of a
wingbeat. Approaching the road, what he *did* hear
was the breath and fidgeting of a human. Small. Cold.
Impatient. Could it be the little one? It was! What was she
doing perched in the hedge? Had she come to find him?
She was trying to be stealthy too, though
of course all the night folk knew she
was there.

18

Spectral Manoeuvres in the Dark

Lil crouched behind the hedge. She'd been there a long time.
One horse had galloped by, but it was only Farmer
Woolpot's son, Jeb. He had slowed his pony to a tentative
trot as he approached the spot where Lil had been hiding,
but all of a sudden he had flicked the reins and urged the
poor creature on at breakneck speed. Lil didn't think he'd
seen her, but she did wonder what he was doing out and
about at this hour.

That had been about half an hour ago, and no one else
had passed. Lil felt sure the highwaymen would have gone
back to the woods by now. But if they had, she hadn't seen
them pass. What if they had gone a different way? No. This

was the quickest route by far. What if they had gone past the spot before she got to her hiding place? . . . Or what if they had gone somewhere else entirely? Lil was beginning to see the gaping flaws in her plan. She was cold and her right foot was wet and numb. Her breath formed a brief warm mist in front of her face, before the wind picked up again and chilled her to the bone. Still she waited.

There it was again. A rustling behind her in the pitch black, closer this time. There was definitely something out there. She shifted her weight slightly. What was she doing

crouched in a bush in the middle of the night, dressed as a dead highwayman? She yawned and shivered. The wind moaned and tugged at her hat. Glancing behind her into the empty field, she strained her eyes to distinguish a dark shape. Just a scarecrow? Something moved at the edge of her vision, over near the hedgerow again.

Scratchy could just make out the little one, though her shape was different tonight. What was she up to? He shook out his feathers, ready to flutter-scoot closer, but his crow senses told him to freeze. Someone else was lurking near the hedge. Sharp claws? A jaw-snapper? He blinked and slowly turned his head, peeking carefully through one eye, then the other. Yes. A jaw-snapper, hunched in the long grass at the edge of the mud. He wanted to hop closer to the little one, but the wily old jaw-snapper was in the way. He kept absolutely still, hoping it hadn't scented him, but he was sure that it had. The jaw-snapper shifted its weight and leaned closer, lifting one black-clawed paw. *Crack.* A snapping branch gave it away. It knew it. It relaxed, knowing the stalking was up. It had lost the element of surprise, it wouldn't

catch its prey this time.
Scratchy leaped into the air,
frantically flapping. The jaw-snapper
pounced half-heartedly, but was
already too late.

There was a crash in the undergrowth and a
snarl. Lil stood up instinctively. Two piercing
eyes spun at her angrily, then blinked away.

A white-tipped tail streaked across the
field and disappeared. Just a fox.

Another scuffling sound. Closer now.
'Who's there?' Lil's voice was small
and shaky.

Silence . . . then a squawk and a fluttering of dark feathers.

'Scratchy? Is that you?'

'*CAAW!*' came the response.

It WAS him!

The fox must have been stalking him. He'd
come back! She hoped he wasn't scared of her
now. Even though she knew he was wild, she
desperately wanted to keep him safe.

He cackled with surprise as her hands closed firmly around his back and belly, clamping his wings to his sides. His fragile, feather-light little body wiggled in her grasp, feet clasping her fingers and beak gripping her hand as she tucked him inside her coat.

'There, there. Calm down. Let's take you back, shall we? Safe and warm. Poor thing . . . you're freezing! You were nearly supper for that fox!'

She abandoned her hiding place. It must be past midnight anyway. Too late for highwaymen now. 'Bother.' She shook her head. She'd have to try again tomorrow night. Maybe in a different spot. But with Ma threatening to sell up, she was running out of time.

'Oh, Scratchy, what are we going to do?' She squelched back around the edge of the muddy field, searching for the fence that followed the track back to the inn. Her too-big boots slopped and sucked at the mud. Ducking under the fence, one of her boots became firmly wedged in the muck. She left it behind, and kicked off the other one too – the sole had flapped off anyway – and made a dash for it in her stockinged feet. The cold mud numbed her toes, and she skittered over the painful gravel as quickly as possible. When she got to the yard, she slowed down. The wind still howled and the sign still squeaked, but she didn't want to risk making a sound. Unlatching the turnip shed, she dodged inside.

'All right, Scratchy. You'll be safe in here. I'm sorry I scared you last night. I didn't mean it.' She slowly released him onto the handle of the turnip shovel.

Scratchy adjusted himself on his familiar perch, puffed his feathers out and hunkered down with his eyes half closed. Lil was shivering, but she carefully stroked his soft velvety head.

'I'll bring you something to eat in the morning. Promise!'

She felt raw with cold. Her fingers were stiff and clumsy, and her feet were frozen. She had completely failed to solve the highwaymen problem, but just for tonight, Lil felt proud and relieved that Scratchy had chosen to come back to her.

He was the best crow ever and she would never let anyone take him away.

Dawn arrived too soon. It had taken a long time for Lil to warm up, and her feet were still as cold as a pair of river trout freshly fished from the pond. She'd been too busy mulling over ideas of how to rid herself, and the inn, of the highwaymen to get much sleep.

'Lil! Come and help your sister get this washing in. You locked up last night – didn't you notice it was still out there?' Ma was up early. That wasn't a good sign.

'No, Ma! Sorry, Ma. Comin'!' Lil shuddered as she threw off her blankets, and raced down the stairs in her nightgown and bare feet.

'What's up with you? You're up late! Are you ill? . . . You 'aven't come down with the lurgy that's laying poor Mr Sprottle low, 'ave you?' It was unusual for Ma to be concerned.

'No, Ma. I'm fine. Just extra tired for some reason.'

'Well, you can't go lazing in bed, young lady, not when there's work to be done!'

'No, Ma.'

Lil was annoyed with herself for sleeping in. She wanted to find something nice to take to Scratchy for his breakfast. It would be much harder to sneak out to him if Ma and Margery were up and on the prowl.

Margery was at one end of the line struggling with a clothes peg, looking miserable. She glanced at Lil and tutted.

'I'll leave you two to it,' Ma announced, pulling her shawl around her shoulders. 'I've got a lot to do today.'

'What is she doing?' Lil asked, once Ma had stepped back into the kitchen.

'More pickles, probably,' said Margery. 'But I reckon she's working herself up to an announcement. I hope it doesn't concern *Mr Boote*. I'd be very happy to have dear Maude as a sister, of course, but I'm not keen on having Arthur traipsing around the place like he owns it. Did you see what he had on his chin yesterday? Silly boy.'

Surely not! Ma and Mr Boote had been toying with the idea of an 'alliance' for years. It would mean marriage, obviously, but Lil had never thought Ma would really go through with it.

'Arthur likes you though . . . ' Lil probed wickedly.

'He does NOT! And even if he did, I wouldn't look at the likes of him! I'm setting my sights much higher than an awkward blacksmith's son. Urgh. Arthur Boote, indeed.'

Lil sniggered.

'What?'

'Nothing.' Lil smirked.

'Don't you dare, you nasty little worm. It's not *my* fault that gentlemen find me enchanting, is it? Arthur's a foolish boy if he thinks he can woo the likes of me.' Margery flapped a sheet aggressively and tossed her hair. 'Anyway, you're just jealous because nobody would look twice at *you*!'

Lil shrugged.

'*Although*... haven't you been spending a lot of time with that *servant* boy... Ed... Ted... whatever his name is?'

'Ned. Yes. He's my friend,' Lil revealed, although she didn't really want to discuss the matter with Margery.

'You can't be friends with a customer's *servant*. That's silly. He won't be here for long, then what are you going to do? Write letters?' Margery scoffed. 'Dear Ned, it's Lil Scroggins 'ere. Still counting pickles and scrubbing out the chamber pots. How's life treating you? Pray, do tell! It must be fascinating, picking nits outta people's wigs!'

'Don't be mean, Margery. It makes you look like a wincing trout.'

'I think Ma *should* sell this place,' Margery continued, ignoring the insult, '*then* we could live in town. That's where all the rich young gentlemen are.'

'We'll be moving to a turnip farm if she sells, Margery, not the big city.'

'*You* might be. You and Arthur. But Maude and me would 'ave a stall, or a shop in town! To sell the pies. We're more presentable, Ma says.'

Lil felt a flutter of panic. 'But things could pick up at the inn, and then we wouldn't be moving anywhere.'

'Fat chance of that! We've been *besieged* by highwaymen! It's terrible for business! Although Eliza Cough-Mannington from the village said that one of them was quite dashing... in a roguish kind of way. *She* said she wouldn't have minded being kidnapped by him.'

'Kidnapped? They're not kidnapping people, Margery. They're robbing people!'

'Tut, whatever! Anyway, I don't see what anyone can do about it, so I reckon The Squawking Mackerel is *doomed*. Besides, I'd like a new bonnet, and I shall be able to buy a nice one if I sell enough pies in town...'

Much as she wanted to argue, Lil had better things to do than stand around flapping laundry with Margery. 'If you say so,' she replied, stacking her pile of sheets and pillow cases into the basket. 'Dump your lot on top, I'll take them in.'

'What?' Margery was surprised by Lil's helpfulness. 'Here you go then.' She piled her own smaller bundle of pillow cases on top of Lil's, chucked the peg bag in, and hurried

off towards the Bootes' cottage. 'I need to talk to Maude,' she called over her shoulder.

Lil sighed. She needed to avoid Ma, get dressed, and grab some breakfast for Scratchy.

She hefted the laundry basket onto her hip and staggered with it into the kitchen and up the stairs. She noticed Ma greeting an elderly gentleman at the front door who looked vaguely familiar. What was she up to?

As soon as the sheets had been deposited in the empty rooms, and Lil was dressed, she raced back downstairs into the kitchen. She hadn't spoken to Ned yet this morning, but first she wanted to feed Scratchy. She ferreted about in the larder for some biscuit crumbs, then found the leftover eel pie and gouged some of the slimy jelly out with a spoon. She added a thick chunk of eel tail on top. It looked particularly unappetising in her hand, but she knew Scratchy would love it.

As she opened the shed door, she was relieved to see him perched on the turnip shovel where she had left him the night before.

'*Caaaw*,' he complained.

'I'm sorry, Scratchy. I got up late, and then I got stuck bringing in yesterday's laundry. I think Ma's up to something and I don't like it. Here you are . . . ' She opened her hand and offered the slimy little pile to him.

'*CAAAW!*' He flapped his wings excitedly and jumped onto her outstretched arm. He had never done that before.

'We have to get rid of Rotten Bob before Ma sells the inn. Much as I don't like living here, I don't want to move. They won't let me take you with me for a start, and then what will happen?'

There was a gentle *tap tap* on the shed door. 'Lil? It's me.'

168

'Come in, Ned,' she whispered.

Ned ducked into the shed and smiled when he saw the crow perched on Lil's arm grappling with a chunk of eel too big to swallow. 'He's back!'

'Yes! I found him last night.'

'That was lucky . . . I knew he'd come back though.' Ned sat on the turnip pile. He looked exhausted. 'Mr Sprottle's staying in bed *again* today. Had me up and down the stairs all night.'

'Oh, no! Is he still in a bad way?'

'Yes. I don't think your ma's medicinal tea is working. Still . . . means I get to stay here a bit longer.'

'Yes!' It was horrible that Ned had to look after Mr Sprottle, but Lil was relieved she would have her friend with her for at least another day.

'So . . . ' Ned paused. 'How did it go last night?'

'Not very well. Apart from finding Scratchy, that is.'

'What happened?'

'Not much. The highwaymen didn't go past. At least not while I was there, hiding in the bushes like an idiot.'

'Maybe they went before you got there? Are you going back out there tonight? You could try a bit earlier . . . or a different spot?'

'No. It was a stupid plan. I can't go lurking in the hedge every night on the off-chance that Rotten Bob will pass by, and I can't go stalking around everywhere in the dark trying to find him!'

'No. I suppose not.' Ned thought for a few moments, then asked hesitantly, 'Is there any way you could *track* him?'

Lil considered it, but she wasn't sure she knew how to track a highwayman, and time was running out. She looked at Scratchy, perched expectantly on her arm hoping for more biscuit crumbs. 'I've got a better idea!' she said suddenly. 'We need to make Rotten Bob come to us.'

'That . . . would work better. But . . . how?' Ned asked, suspiciously.

'I'm not sure yet. But I'll think of something,' she replied.

Five more carriages were accosted by highwaymen that day; three of them were held up twice! And the Eggy Bottom mud slick ensured that they had *all* ended up jostling for attention at the inn.

Judging by the distressed state of that day's customers, Lil's storytelling had had little effect on the remaining highwaymen. The descriptions of the gang matched what Lil had seen of Bob and his friends at the camp a few nights

ago. They seemed determined to stick to this particular patch of road and, unfortunately for the inn, had increased their rate of robbing.

Tale after tale of 'The Dread Highwayman Robert Hatchet', as Rotten Bob now called himself, circulated the lounge, and the coach drivers talked continually about him out in the back parlour.

'*Bob* was a giant.'

'*Bob* was a crack shot.'

'*Bob* could hold up two coaches at once.'

'*Bob* was so fast he could run down the mail coach!'

Worse still were the stories making him out to be some kind of purse-snatching hero.

'Bob was always polite to the *ladies*.' (Lil doubted that very much!)

'Bob was a wrongfully-accused fugitive, forced into a life of crime.' (Nonsense.)

'Bob gave half of what he stole to the poor.' (Absolute codswallop!)

Where did people get such ridiculous ideas from? Lil tried to counter the growing rumours of Rotten Bob with her own stories of Ghastly Jack Crowheart.

'It seems to me that this *Robert Hatchet* is nowhere near as scary as Ghastly Jack Crowheart,' Lil said knowingly to a woman dressed in mourning clothes who'd been travelling to hear her uncle's will read. 'What with Jack being a ghost and all that. A proper ghoul he is, stalking the woods howling, "Tell me her naaaaaaame . . ."'

'Lil Scroggins!' shrieked Ma. 'Stop with your nonsense *right* this minute! Don't you think it's bad enough with *real*

highwaymen ruining my business, without you adding to it?'

Ma had good enough hearing when it suited her. Lil shrugged and stomped off to the back parlour.

''Ere, Lil,' Mr Boote called to her as she slunk past. He was sitting in his usual spot, tucking in to Ma's disgusting pastries. 'Fred Woolpot's lad, Jeb, reckons he saw *something strange* in the hedge last night. Didn't stop to find out what it was, but I reckon it might have been your *crowman*!'

'Demon highwayman,' Lil corrected. 'It could have been Ghastly Jack, yes. He *is* said to haunt that particular stretch of road.'

'Well, either way,' Mr Boote continued, 'I heard young Jeb rode into the village all of a f*lutter*. In a right tiddle he was, horse well lathered up too! Maybe he'd been at his father's ale!' He snorted.

They weren't taking it seriously. It made Lil furious. Why should that windbag Bob steal all the glory? He was just a loud-mouthed bully, taking advantage of people just because he could!

'I'm sorry. Shouldn't laugh,' Mr Boote continued in between snorts. 'Not very good for your ma's business, is it? All them highwaymen? Once a place gets a reputation, well, there's not much you can do 'bout it!' He took

another bite of pastry and grinned cheerfully. Lil turned
to walk away. 'Don't you worry though, lass,' he called
after her with his mouth full. 'Your ma and me might
come to *an arrangement* soon.'

I sincerely hope not, thought Lil.

Things were getting desperate.

19

Daylight Robbery

'Stand and deliver!'

The horses whinnied and reared as the coachman hauled on the reins. Rotten Bob Hatchet – or rather *Robert* Hatchet as he was now known, stood in his own horse's stirrups with Blasty Bess pointed at the carriage. His horse snorted unhappily and pawed the road.

'All right, all right! We don't want any trouble!' yelled the coachman, raising his hands shakily into the air.

Bob's horse began to skitter and walk sideways, objecting to its clumsy treatment. Bob yanked on the bit in its mouth but that made the horse toss its head and shake its mane even more. He plonked himself back into the saddle and pulled

tight on the reins.

It was a new horse. Bought with the proceeds of his recent crimes. He'd decided he needed a faster, sleeker mount. It was a shame he couldn't ride the poor beast properly.

'Out the carriage!' Bob shouted at the unseen occupants of the curtained interior. It was a fine coach, all shiny brass fittings and polished wood. 'Come on! I 'avent got all day!'

Bob walked his horse slowly around the carriage. A latch clicked and the door began to rattle as a passenger struggled to open it with shaking hands. At last it swung wide and a velvet-clad foot cautiously poked out.

'We are unarmed!' came the trembling voice from inside. 'You may take our purse, but pray, leave us unharmed...'

'Out you come, first... then I'll put Blasty Bess 'ere away. Do yerself a favour and get on with it!' Bob had walked his horse to the side of the carriage now, but it wouldn't settle. He gripped hard with his knees, and struggled to keep Blasty Bess level as he pointed the gun at the unfortunate gentleman climbing out of the carriage.

'That's it. Out you come. Hands up in the air where I can see them.'

The man was quite young with a high forehead, impressive wig and immaculately rouged cheeks. A small lace handkerchief fluttered in his fingers as he nervously held his arms above his head.

'And the rest of you . . . come on, out you get!'

Bob had hit the jackpot. This lot were clearly the richest mugs he'd held up all day.

'It's my mother! She has a very delicate disposition. Please . . . here . . . take *my* purse. There's more than enough in it to get you . . . whatever it is that you want.'

'Do you know who I am?' Rotten Bob barked. 'I don't care about your mother's disposition, I told 'er to GET OUT!'

'Let me help her,' quaked a young girl's voice from behind the curtain. There was a shifting of carriage springs. The little door thwacked open again and a drabbly dressed girl scurried out backwards, stumbling into the mud. She straightened herself and then offered her arm to a lace glove that gripped it like the talons of a vulture. Heavy black skirts came next, then another velveteen foot hovered from the doorway. Shakily the ancient woman creaked to the ground, her thin dash of a mouth furious beneath a narrow veiny nose and squinting wrinkled eyes. The small girl settled her mistress onto a walking stick and scuttled round to support her other arm.

'Who's this?' Bob gestured to the girl.

'The maid . . .' replied the gentleman as if the matter were obvious, '. . . and my foot boy.' Another even smaller young boy jumped out of the carriage and stood quietly by the door.

'Right, so . . . all of yer, *hands up*!' Bob demanded.

'Oi, Frank, get over 'ere and give me an 'and with this lot, will yer!'

Swanky Frank du Bonnet came scrambling from the other side of the hedge, followed by Three-Fingered Ted.

'Where's Martin?' Bob asked.

'He's stalking crows, I think.'

'Well, keep your eye on this lot for me while I get off me 'orse.' Bob shifted in the saddle and started to rock back and forth. The horse snorted loudly. Bob launched himself to the ground. The horse whinnied and stamped and began to back away when Bob grabbed the reins again. 'Stay 'ere and keep still!' he snarled. 'Ted, come over 'ere and hold my horse, will you? I swear the stupid nag is up to something.' He brushed himself off, adjusted his cravat, and strode towards his captives. As he came face to face with the terrified gentleman, he gave Blasty Bess a whirl around his finger, uncocked the hammer

and tucked the gun back into his belt. 'No need for Blasty Bess here, eh? I don't expect any *unpleasantries*. Only a fool would trifle with the Dread Highwayman Robert Hatchet, eh?'

All four of his captives nodded anxiously.

'So! What have you got for me then? Frank . . . search them!'

'Yes, Bob!' Frank swaggered over to the group with an appraising eye. 'Pockets?' he enquired with a clipped accent.

'Two at the sides and one in the back,' the gentleman replied.

Frank dug in the man's heavily embroidered jacket pockets and brought out a finely engraved silver snuff box and a heavy purse. He handed them to Bob, who tested the weight of the purse by chucking it up and down. Bob nodded towards the gentleman again. 'And the rest,' he growled.

The gentleman cautiously lowered one hand and opened the side of his jacket to reveal his blue silken waistcoat. Frank grabbed the watch chain that hung from the inside breast pocket and fished out a gold watch that glinted in the sunshine. He flicked it open and showed it to Bob. 'Nice!' he appraised. The man whimpered.

'How are we doing for jewellery?' Bob asked Frank conversationally.

'I shall take a closer look,' said Frank cheerfully. He inspected the older woman's earrings, then took out a magnifying glass to look at the large emeralds hung about her neck. 'These do seem to be of a suitable quality, Bob,' he reported.

'I should think so too. Only the best for Robert Hatchet,' Bob chuckled. 'Madam?'

The woman gasped and fumbled with the necklace at her throat. Her freckle-faced maid darted forward, bobbing her knees to the woman, then to Bob, then to the woman again, before helping her to undo the clasp. She stood wide-eyed with the necklace in her palm, and glanced between her elderly mistress and Bob. Frank swooped in and snatched the prize from her grasp. 'Thank you, kindly,' he chattered. 'And the earrings!'

The woman whined as her maid carefully removed her sparkling earrings and dropped them into Frank's outstretched hand.

'There! Wasn't so bad, was it?' crooned Bob. The captives relaxed a fraction and the boy turned to help his master back into the carriage.

'Er, not so fast.' Bob pocketed the necklace and earrings. 'I didn't say you could leave, did I?' The boy froze and shook his head, squirming to suddenly find himself the focus of Bob's menacing attention.

'I said, DID I?' Bob repeated.

'No!' yelped the boy, turning helplessly to the gentleman, who looked away.

'Are you an *honest* lad, lad?' Bob enquired.

'Y-y-yes!' came the squeaked response.

'Then *what* will be *your* contribution to this friendly transaction? A bright boy like *you* must 'ave a few pennies squirrelled away, surely?'

The boy opened his mouth to protest, but Bob loomed over him and held his massive dirty hand out in front of the boy's nose. The boy stared wide-eyed for a few moments until Bob raised a questioning eyebrow. The boy sighed and rummaged in his back pocket. He reluctantly brought out his hand and opened his palm to reveal two shiny shillings. His life savings.

Bob slapped his thigh and roared with laughter. 'An honest lad indeed!' he bellowed, snatching the shillings and dropping them into his pocket. Bob had no need of a few measly shillings, not after the haul he'd just made, but he enjoyed the misery he inflicted upon others. 'Go on then, you lot. Off you go. Get out of my sight!' He flapped at the carriage, dismissing his victims with glee.

The coachman wasted no time in getting going. He clicked his teeth and tapped the lead horse on the rump. Soon the carriage was trundling along the bumpy road at a brisk trot.

'Do you reckon that wiggy bloke had another purse on 'im?' grumbled Ted. 'I bet he did!'

'Of course he did!' smirked Bob. 'We'll have another go at 'im round the corner! Come on, mount up, we'll be across that field and waiting for them to come round the bend.'

He strutted towards Ted, who was still wrestling to control Bob's new horse. 'Ha! There's no escape from the

Dread Highwayman Robert Hatchet. I've made quite a name for meself. Famous from 'ere to London, me. Infamous, even! I'm a legend, I am! 'Ere, keep that 'orse still, I'm tryin' to get back on it.'

Bob pulled on the bridle and hopped about as he tried to wedge his boot into the stirrup. The horse grunted and swished its tail angrily. After several attempts he succeeded in winching himself awkwardly into the saddle and tugged on the reins. Again the horse skittered sideways, until Bob kicked his heels into its flanks and snapped the reins.

'Giddy up, ya four-legged louse!' The stallion neighed in distress and reared up briefly before striking the

THU

ground and kicking up clods of dirt and gravel. The rest of the gang scrambled for their own horses as Bob spurred his mount at speed across the lumpy field, shouting directions. After a few strides, the tormented horse veered towards a low branch.

There was a loud thunk as Bob hit the ground and his horse galloped on, unencumbered, up the hill.

Drastic Measures

Ma called a family meeting. She announced that Mr Crankshaw the cart-maker was interested in acquiring the inn so that he could pull it down to make room for a timber yard. So that was who Lil had seen the previous morning! Ma also declared that she had another prospective buyer coming over to look round the place the following day, and that they had better tidy the place up so she could get a better price for it than what Mr Crankshaw was offering. Lil tried to protest, but Ma was adamant.

'What am I supposed to do with a collection of old bedroom slippers and "I owe you" letters?' she complained. 'If this place can't turn a profit, it'll 'ave to go!'

At least there was no announcement concerning Mr Boote. Lil was thankful for that, but she was furious about Rotten Bob. He was ruining everything! It was clear that getting rid of him before Ma sold the inn would require a more *drastic* plan. But what could one small girl do against a big bully like him? Bob was a real-life villain, and a vicious and dangerous one at that. Perhaps Ned was right, and she'd only make things worse with her meddling. But she couldn't let him win. As she carried a heavy tray of chinking ale mugs out to the cellar, Lil wished she was bigger. As big as Ghastly Jack Crowheart, even. But if Lil Scroggins couldn't do anything about Rotten Bob, then maybe the demon highwayman could?

And that meant Ghastly Jack had to get real. Really real.

That evening the Bishop was back. He had wisely travelled along the Eggy Bottom detour rather than brave the mud on the main road again. There was no mention of highwaymen, but Lil doubted he would have put up with any nonsense from a bunch of ruffians anyway. Besides, the

Bishop was armed. He travelled with his own fire power in
the form of an ancient but formidable blunderbuss that he
kept propped on the seat beside him. The Bishop's coach
was pulled by a sleek team of four and driven by his trusty
footman Choakes. Choakes *never* came into the inn.
Apparently, he preferred to stay out in the stables with the
horses and kip in the carriage. Lil would usually take him a
bowl or two of whatever the Bishop had leftover, but he
never spoke a word. Choakes was a huge man with big
hunched shoulders and red-rimmed eyes. Lil didn't suppose

he slept much. He also wore a
vast moth-ridden cape that covered
his massive frame like a tent. And it was
that cape which gave Lil a brilliant idea ... if
she could only persuade him to let her borrow it.

'I've got another idea,' she told Ned. 'And I'm going
to need your help again.'

Ned blinked.

'I need you to pretend to be one of Ghastly Jack's victims.
I was thinking...if we tied you to a tree, and you were, you
know...screaming...that would attract Rotten Bob's
attention.'

Lil outlined her ingenious new plan, while Ned stood
with a look of horror upon his face.

'It's an airtight plan, Ned. Trust me. What could possibly
go wrong?'

Ned considered the many terrifying and catastrophic
things that were extremely likely to go wrong with Lil's plan.

It ran against all his instincts and was definitely *not* the
sort of thing Snederick Smythe should be getting involved
with under *any* circumstances. It was dangerous and risky
and scary, and what's more, even if he *didn't* die at the hands
of a mob of cutthroats, he'd get in *massive* trouble with

Mr Sprottle. Mr Sprottle would send him home to his family in disgrace, and then his own parents would disown him! But somehow, despite the certain danger, he knew he was going to do it. How could he not? Lil was the first friend he had ever had, and it was this fact alone which made him even *consider* such reckless behaviour.

'All right,' he said. 'I'll do it.'

He felt sick.

21

A Fraudulent Parrot

When the inn was finally silent for the night, Lil and Ned gathered the props they had prepared and snuck out of the back door. The door was under Ma's bedroom so they needed to be extra stealthy when leaving, but it made sense to go that way since Lil needed to make a quiet detour to the stables. As Lil approached, she saw Scratchy jump onto the hitching post to watch her. He would be coming along on this little adventure and she hoped he would be quiet as they made their way to the spot where she intended to spring her trap.

As she entered
the stables, the horses whickered
and shifted in their stalls. 'Easy there,' she whispered softly.
Choakes had drawn the little carriage up under the yard roof
as he usually did. Lil tiptoed towards it and peered inside.
A great motionless shape leaned against the back seat. Was
Choakes asleep?

'Choakes? Are you awake?' she whispered. 'I've brought

you the quilts, like I promised.' The shape shifted and sat up. Lil held up the bundle of quilts that she had selected from the lost property cupboard. Choakes narrowed his eyes at first, but to her relief he shrugged off his enormous cape and handed it through the carriage window to her. 'Thank you, Choakes – I'll bring it back to you by morning, promise on my life!' A glimmer of a smile played across his face, and then he spread the quilts out, leaned back and closed his eyes. Her plan was all set.

'When we get to the woods, we'll have to creep. We don't want them to hear anything until we're ready,' Lil whispered.

Ned nodded. He was utterly petrified, and as the cold night air and the even colder realisation of what he was about to do hit him, he considered backing out altogether.

Lil led the way, with Scratchy flittering from fence post to hedge along the open road. They were probably safe from being overheard out here, but somehow it felt right to whisper and move stealthily, keeping a wary eye out for any late-night travellers.

'Lil! What was that?' Ned quickened his pace to catch up with her, peering wide-eyed over the top of the large bundle he carried.

'Probably a fox . . . or a badger,' Lil replied, feigning confidence. She had no idea what dangerous animals might be following them along the road. Still, it felt safer with Ned and Scratchy along for the ride. At least she wasn't on her own this time.

'What if it's one of *them*?' Ned worried.

'I doubt it. They'll all be camped up for the night in the woods. It's just . . . things. You know. Night things. Going about their business.'

Talking seemed to help calm Ned's nerves. And her own.

'I'm a bit worried about Scratchy. I hope he doesn't fly off and get lost or gobbled up,' she chattered. 'He's not meant to be out at night.'

'Do you think he'll stay perched on your shoulder? You know, when it's time in your plan?' asked Ned.

'Hopefully. I've brought some crumbs with me to persuade him.'

They continued in silence for a few moments, but Lil could tell that Ned wanted to ask her something.

'I keep meaning to ask you,' he said at last.

'What?'

'Well... the inn sign. It doesn't make any sense, does it? Why does it have a parrot on it if the inn's called The Squawking Mackerel?'

'Ha! There's a story to that,' Lil explained. 'When the inn was first built, a long time before Ma owned it, some old scallywag who *said* he was a pirate stayed at the inn with his pet parrot. The people at the inn had never seen a parrot before and when they asked him what it was, the old trickster told them it was a mackerel.'

'Why?' Ned laughed.

'I've no idea. He was pulling their leg I guess,' Lil

continued, 'but anyway, they'd never seen a mackerel or a parrot, so they believed him. *And*, because it was probably the most exciting thing that had ever happened to them in their sorry little lives, they renamed the inn "The Squawking Mackerel". The name's just stuck since then.'

'How could anyone not know what a parrot is?'

'I don't know, but can you see what I mean about this place? It's why I want to travel the world when I'm older, and I certainly don't want to end up on some backwater turnip farm!'

Scratchy crashed through the top of a shrub and skittered to a halt on the road in front of Lil. He cawed sheepishly, trying to recover his dignity. After strolling wonkily up and down for a moment, he flapped up to sit atop the bundle of props Lil was carrying.

'What have you been up to, you daft thing? You'll wake the whole neighbourhood up if you carry on like that.'

'Maybe something frightened him! I don't like it out here at night, Lil. It feels . . . ominous.'

'Look, see where that branch is sticking up against the sky, that's where we can get into the woods. Come on. We'll have to be extra careful once we get inside. I'm banking on Rotten Bob and his mob being tucked up in their camp, but I don't know where they'll be for sure. We'll head towards the hollowed-out tree where the crows roost. There's nearly a full moon, so we'll be able to find our way.'

22

Into the Woods

Ned barely managed to keep his nerve as he and Lil moved as silently as possible through the trees. He had never really been the outdoors type. His job had always kept him safely inside, traipsing along with Mr Sprottle in a whirlwind of corsets and oversized undergarments. He could navigate the social perils of the stuffy world he moved in, but brambles and nettles and creepy crawlies were quite another prospect. Lil seemed oblivious to the wildness of it all as she strode ahead, holding back brambles and bracken for him, and directing where he should put his feet so that a branch didn't snap back and swipe him in the face.

Scratchy was excited. He perched on top of the bundle

that the little one was carrying so that he could see what she could see. They were going a long slow route through the trees because the humans were so big and stuck on the ground, but this time he wasn't afraid of the snapping teeth and snatching claws. This time the little one was with him, and the jaw-snappers and flying screechers were afraid of *her*. As she stamped and crunched through the leaves, he could tell that the little one and her friend were up to something. They stopped near the lightning tree where the big crows roosted. They were planning a trick. Hiding things in the leaves. He watched for a while, peering through one eye then the other, but soon spotted a big juicy snail peeking from its shell and decided to hunt instead.

Hidden beneath a vast cloak of shadows, high in a tree scoured white from lightning strikes, a hundred crows had sworn revenge. Hunched in half-sleep, one eye awake to the moon's glimmer reflected off scudding clouds, they fluffed their inky feathers against the chill and waited. A chittering noise rumbled in and out of the branches: '… the Nasty Faces must go … the Nasty Faces must go …'

Brothers and sisters had been lost. Cruelly killed. Unfairly tricked. The big stinker had taken a wicked toll. Anger

rippled through the flock. A hundred night black eyes kept watch through creaking branches.

23

Trappings

Lil dumped her bundle onto the wet mossy ground.

'Right. This'll do,' she said.

Ned let his own heavy bundle slip to the floor and looked around the clearing. A twig snapped to his left and he caught sight of something darting into the brambles.

'That's where we'll tie you up,' whispered Lil.

Ned screwed up his face and tramped quietly to the gnarled twisted tree trunk.

'All right,' he replied.

'But first, let's set up the frying pan and the Bishop's blunderbuss. Look, we can hang the pan from that branch and bury the blunderbuss in those leaves underneath. If I stand

on this side I should be able to cut the knicker elastic before anyone knows what I'm up to.'

'All right,' said Ned again. He wasn't convinced about this part of the plan at all. 'But what if it explodes too soon?'

'It doesn't have any shot in it, just the gunpowder. And I'll have the heavy cape on to protect me from the blast.'

Ned carried the sooty iron pan over to the tree and held it up to Lil, who nimbly climbed up the tree trunk and shimmied along the branch. She wrapped the knicker elastic around the branch and then dangled one end down to Ned who tied it to the pan handle.

'Right. Hold that up,' she said, jumping down to land in the leaves with a muffled thud.

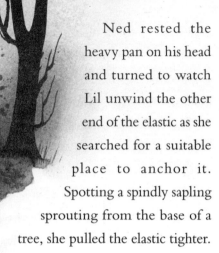

Ned rested the heavy pan on his head and turned to watch Lil unwind the other end of the elastic as she searched for a suitable place to anchor it. Spotting a spindly sapling sprouting from the base of a tree, she pulled the elastic tighter.

'This will have to be under great tension,' she explained, pulling the elastic further and further towards the sapling until the pan began to lift. 'It needs to fall from the full height of that branch. Right, come over here and help me tie it off. I can barely hold on to it!'

Ned cautiously let go of the pan. It lurched downwards and sprung a few times before settling. It hung halfway between the branch and the ground and spun in one direction then the other. Ned sighed and went to help Lil.

They both pulled the elastic and slowly the iron pan hitched higher and higher until it dangled just beneath the branch. The elastic cut into their hands but Ned braced himself against the tree stump while Lil pulled a tight knot

around the base of the sapling. Then they let go.

The sapling whipped taut and several layers of leaves were stripped from its base as the elastic jerked to the point where it became wedged.

The whole arrangement stretched across the edge of the clearing like a high tension tightrope. Both pan and sapling rocked to and fro as if they were on opposite ends of a see-saw. Lil gently prodded the taut elastic. Ned flinched.

'Do you think Mr Sprottle's *remarkably modern knicker elastic* is strong enough to hold?' he asked.

'If it can hold up Lady Austerely-Perch's bloomers then it should have no trouble suspending a frying pan.'

'I'm not sure if I want to be the one to test it out. How are we going to bury the blunderbuss under it? What if it snaps too soon?'

'Don't worry,' said Lil. 'I'll do it. Help me scoop up some leaves to add to the pile.'

The Bishop's blunderbuss was as temperamental as its owner. She had quietly borrowed it while he snored into his soup at supper. If he ever found out she'd taken it, she'd be done for.

Lil unwrapped the ornate gun and placed it gingerly on the ground beside her. She stretched her arms to clear a patch

of leaves, keeping out of the direct line of drop, in case the frying pan should suddenly land on her head. The ground was mulchy and rife with scurrying and wriggling life. Scratchy hopped up and down next to her and darted in to jab his shiny black beak at the bugs.

'Come on, Scratchy, out the way. It's not a game.'

Scratchy looked at Lil with one eye then the other. He stalked casually round to the other side of the earthy patch, grabbed a snail, and took off to a nearby bush.

Lil carefully positioned the blunderbuss underneath the dangling pan and pushed the dirt and leaf litter back on top. Ned deposited another armful of brown leaf mulch as Lil swished it around.

'There. You'd never know.' She got back to her feet and stood admiring her handiwork. 'Right then. Now it's time to bring Ghastly Jack to life.'

She untied the knot in the bundle she had been carrying and spread the manky old cape on the ground. There was a waft of stale armpits. 'Panniers first, I reckon.'

Ned snapped all the rivets open and assembled the frame. It wasn't the biggest set of panniers that Mr Sprottle stocked, those ones were wider than a carriage and would have looked silly. This pair was about the width of a good-sized doorway.

Ned held them up and Lil poked her head through the middle, so that they rested on her shoulders.

'I'll fasten the ribbons under your arms like this so that it doesn't wobble so much. You won't be able to tell under the cape. Check you can still move your arms,' he said. He was an expert at scaffolding these contraptions.

Next came the make-up. Lil smeared her face with the white greasy paste, and then crumbled the charcoal into her hands and wiped them down the hollows of her cheeks. She patted it all around her chin to create a kind of undead stubble. Ned opened the small pot of rouge and dabbed it about her eyes.

'This is an expensive brand, you know.'

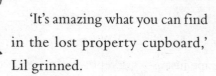

'It's amazing what you can find in the lost property cupboard,' Lil grinned.

'I'm not sure about the wig, though. It looks like a trampled doormat.'

'Don't worry, I'll pull the collar up and stick the hat on top. It's properly dark now so they won't see me clearly.' They draped the heavy coachman's cape over the panniers.

The trickiest part of the disguise was balancing on the stilts. They'd been Ned's idea. After fixing up the panniers to make Lil look wider, he had set about finding a way to make her taller too. At the back of the turnip shed, they had found an old butter churn that had lost its plunger, and a broken feed bucket behind the stables. They had then hunted along the fence posts for rusty nails that Ned could use to fix a mismatched pair of lost property boots to the upturned bottoms of the churn and bucket. They were uneven heights, but Lil could mainly stand on the upside-down churn and just use the rickety bucket for balance. With any luck she wouldn't need to do much walking about. Ned tied Lil's feet tightly into the ragged boots, wrapping extra string around the ankles, and helped her to stand up on her wobbly new feet. As Lil carefully straightened up to her full height, the cape just about swept the floor.

The glove came next. Ned found a longish stick and arranged the tattered white glove on the end to form a skeletal hand. Lil tucked the other end inside the cape and waved the hand around like Mr Sprottle describing one of his inventions.

Last of all, Ned upended the pot of wig powder and threw handfuls of it all over Lil, lending the hat and the cape a dusty ethereal glow. Lil coughed through the puffs.

'All right. That's enough. How do I look?'

'Horrible,' Ned grimaced. 'Can you walk on those things?'

'Yes. Well. Kind of.' Lil took a few lurching steps. 'I don't have far to go. Now hold on to my stick arm for me, while I tie you to the tree. We need to hurry up.'

Poor Ned shuddered as he took his position against the misshapen tree trunk. The branches were warped and bent into twisted forms. It looked every bit the 'Crow Tree' of Lil's spooky tale. Scratchy flew to a stub on one of its ancient gnarled branches and flapped his wings in practice.

'What if the crows really *do* come and peck out my eyes?'

'They won't! They're asleep! That's why we need the loud bang to get them cawing. Anyway, the story's all made up, Ned. They won't *really* hurt you!'

Lil's assurances did nothing to alleviate Ned's fear. 'I don't like spiders either, Lil . . . I hope this doesn't take too long. There's creepy crawlies all over this tree.'

'I'm sorry, Ned. With any luck they'll get an eyeful of Ghastly Jack and leg it. You won't have to be tied up for too long. Do you remember your lines?'

'Yes. I . . . I think so.'

'All right then. Let me get hidden behind this bush, and I'll make my entrance once Rotten Bob arrives.' Lil was aware that she was asking a lot of someone she didn't know that well. Poor Ned.

Another sliver of moon peeked through the cloud, just enough to cast a silvery half-light through the trees, stretching the shadows and obscuring any traces of Lil's trap.

Ned closed his eyes. There was no turning back now. He took a deep breath, then let loose the most dreadful anguished scream he could manage. He howled and wailed in terror. He wasn't exactly *acting*. His desperate pleas for rescue carried through the eerie moonlight and haunted the entire wood.

24

The Nasty Faces

I t was a good twenty minutes before Rotten Bob's gang
came crashing and stumbling through the undergrowth.
Lil had heard them approaching, and it was clear they were
being coaxed along by threats. Any sensible person would
have run away from Ned's horrifying screams. He'd nearly
gone hoarse from all the yelling.

'Wos going on 'ere then?' exclaimed Rotten Bob as he
clattered into the clearing with his pistol drawn.

'Hell's bells, Bob, it's the Crow Tree! Like in the story!
Let's get out of here!' Swanky Frank wasn't keen on having
an encounter with anything unusual in the woods.

'Hold up, you load of lily-livered cowherds. Let's find

out what's going on first.' Bob tucked Blasty Bess back into
his belt and strode to the centre of the clearing. 'Look, it's just
a boy tied to a tree! Making an awful racket for a scrawny
little tiddler an' all.'

Ned was genuinely terrified. It took an enormous effort
to focus on his lines and not faint.

'Run, sirs! Save yourselves!' he whimpered.

'You was just screaming for help a minute ago?'

'Er. I was. But I can't be saved. Not now. Not from
Ghastly Jack.'

'Ghastly Jack?' gasped Ted. 'You don't mean . . . Ghastly
Jack Crowheart the *Demon Highwayman*?'

'Yes. That's him.' Ned nodded. 'He's a terrible ghoul and
he keeps asking me this same question *over* and *over* again!'

Lil ducked behind the bush and held the rolled up newspaper to her mouth. She hoped this would send the silly scoundrels packing with their tails between their legs.

'Tell me her naaaaaaame!' she moaned, her disembodied voice made sinister and menacing in the dark.

'Crikey, Bob! You hear that?' Monstrous Martin backed away from the sound.

'Now, Bob . . . seriously, mate. We should be off,' stuttered Ted.

'Tell me her naaAAAAAME!' Lil boomed through the makeshift trumpet.

'This is some severely spooky shenanigans 'ere, Bob.' Swanky Frank was quaking in his boots. 'I'd say we should scarper.'

'AAAAARGH!' wailed Ned. 'He's behind you!'

The highwaymen spun around, and there, peering at them through the murk of the trees was a ghoulish white face hovering in the shrubbery. Lil was wobbling and wavering on her stilts.

'Oh my good crikey me!' Swanky Frank took off at a sprint, and the others made to follow him, jostling each other out of the way.

'Hold up, you lot . . . git back 'ere!' shrieked Bob. 'W-w-we

don't know it's dangerous!' The big bully stood his ground, and although he was visibly trembling, he edged a few steps closer to the ghastly apparition. ''Ere, Ted. You got a knack with things of the uncanny persuasion. 'Ave a word with it, will ya?'

Ted crept back reluctantly, and addressed the ghoul from
behind Bob's shoulder.

'What does you want from us?' he keened in a silly high-
pitched voice. 'Is there anybody theeeerre?'

'Of course there's somebody there, you daft apeth. He's
standing right in front of us. Now get out the way and let
me talk to it.' Bob took another hesitant step forward. 'What
do you want?' he shouted, a little too loudly.

Lil slowly emerged from behind the bush and raised her
spectral stick arm. She pointed directly at Bob.

'Er . . . I'm sorry, Bob . . . You're on yer own with this
one.' Ted quivered as he backed hastily away to where the
others were standing.

Swanky Frank and Monstrous Martin were hovering on the edge of the clearing alongside the few of Bob's gang who remained, torn between the urge to run, and the need to obey Bob's orders. The urge to run was winning out.

Sensing he was about to lose control of his entire gang, Rotten Bob plucked up his courage and reasserted his usual swagger. 'Now, hang on you lot. It's a ghost init? It can't *do* anything to us.'

Lil drew back the elastic on her slingshot and fired off a small dumpling. It hit Bob square on the forehead.

'Waaaaaaaah!' wailed Martin and several of the gang scrambled off into the woods.

Bob staggered back, rubbing his head. 'Oi, what was that for?' he complained. 'We wasn't to know you'd be out 'ere in the woods, pestering some poor mug, was we? Otherwise we'd 'ave left you alone.' He gestured to his trembling comrades. 'You can't blame a chap for exercising his right to a bit of robbing on a fine evening, can you?'

'I'm Ghaaaastly Jack Crowheart, scourge of the roads. Get off my patch before I feed you to my crows.' Lil spoke in a low raspy hiss. It was the only

way she could disguise her voice without the rolled-up newspaper.

'Wos that?' asked Bob, hooking a hand behind his ear. 'You want *us* to shift off this lucrative patch? You got to be joking, mate.'

'No joking for the deeeaaad,' Lil moaned slowly, rummaging in her pocket and edging awkwardly around the bushes to get closer to the elastic suspending the frying pan.

''Ere what are you up to?' snarled Bob. He strode a few steps closer, cutting off Lil's route. 'There's summink *funny* about you,' he pondered, squinting at the immense black shape billowing in front of him, all looming and dank and dreadful. It was wearing a hideous wig that looked like it had been buried in a cupboard for the best part of a decade. Bob crept a tentative step closer.

Scratchy flapped to Lil's shoulder in a scramble of black feathers and began cawing at Bob loudly. The other highwaymen wailed in terror. Ned began to whimper.

'I'll feed you to my croooooooows!' Lil growled. She was finding it very

difficult to stagger about the undergrowth in the stilts and cape whilst keeping her deathly demeanour. She was glad of Scratchy's intervention. Surely his cawing would make Bob back away? But to her dismay he stood his ground.

'Yes, yes, full of it, ain't you, you old bacon-faced bagpipe!' he sneered, crossing his arms, taunting her.

Lil shuffled forwards – but not too far, and raised her spectral stick arm again. 'Raaaaaaahhhhhh!' she roared as scarily as she could.

'For goodness' sake, stop riling it up, Bob!' shrieked Swanky Frank.

'Leave it, Bob!' warbled Ted. 'Come on, let's get out of here while we still can!'

But Bob wouldn't give in. He stood with his hands on his hips defiantly.

'You can bark at the moon all you like, you oversized pair of bellows, but what do you say to a proper fight, eh? Settle this the gentlemanly way, like *real* highwaymen?'

'Oh no, Bob, don't!' wailed Martin. 'Not a duel!'

25

The Challenge

Rotten Bob nodded his head. 'But of course. Only way to settle it. I, Rotten Bob Hatchet, challenge *you* Ghastly Jack Crowheart, to a duel!'

Lil froze – what could she do? She wasn't armed to fight a duel! Rotten Bob was between her and the blunderbuss. Even if she *could* grab the thing and get it to work, there was no shot in it. It would just be an empty bang. But it was all she had to defend herself. She had put herself – and poor Ned – in *terrible* danger. This had been a silly idea from the start. Who was she to take on a grown highwayman? With Ned tied up, her only hope was to keep Bob talking long enough to creep closer to the elastic. But she had run out of

things to say. She edged around the clearing as best she could.

'Oh no, you don't!' ranted Bob. 'Trying to swap places and get the moon in my eyes, are you? Think you can give yourself the advantage, eh? I know all the tricks in the book. We'll do it as we stand.' He turned to the remnants of his quivering gang: 'Frank, begin the count, will ya!'

Scratchy leaped off her shoulder and flew off into the bushes.

Thanks for the vote of confidence, Lil thought. But she couldn't blame him. She'd brought this all on herself. She was seriously considering her chances if she simply gave up, pulled off her disguise and owned up to her trick. Maybe she could beg Bob to let Ned go at least.

Scratchy saw the little one looking at the spot where her trick was buried. The big stinker was in the way. She was cawing at him, *CAAW CHITTER CAAW*, and Scratchy had joined in, but the big stinker stood his ground and cawed back. They couldn't mob the big stinker on their own. He was too big.

Scratchy knew there was a banger stick hidden in the leaves. That must be her trick. He was afraid of the bang, but he knew it would wake the big crows. And then surely they could mob the big stinker together.

He flew to the stretchy worm string the little one had tied to a baby tree, eyeing it with one eye, then the other. It was too tough for him to snap because it was not a real worm. But Scratchy was a clever crow. He had a plan of his own. He scratched and dug at the roots and soil until the little tree started to move.

'Ten paces each and then we turn and draw, got it? Ha, ha! I reckon this might be Ghastly Jack's last stand, you windy old bog-badgerer.'

As Bob continued to threaten and sling insults at her, Lil caught sight of a rustling movement in the undergrowth near the sapling she had tied the frying pan to.

It was Scratchy.

He was jumping from side to side, pulling at something. The elastic! The pan behind Bob dropped a notch as the sapling anchoring it in place began to lift. *Oh Scratchy*, she thought, *if ever you could scrape and peck and destroy something, now is the time to do it!* He hadn't abandoned her after all. He'd set to work with his strong shiny beak and was scratching and

tearing at the ground with his sharp claws. She knew he had little chance of snapping through the elastic itself but if he could uproot the sapling it was attached to, the result would be the same!

Rotten Bob blustered on: 'Swanky Frank du Bonnet here will count us down and be the judge of the duel.'

'Er . . . Bob? I . . . I don't know about that . . . I . . . I mean Master Ghastly here might not *respond* to the conventional effects of a pistol . . . er . . . him being a ghost, and all that . . . it . . . it might be wiser to give in on this particular point.' Frank's voice trembled as he inched further away from the confrontation unfolding in front of him.

'Nonsense!' Bob chuckled. 'Besides, *he* can't back out once a challenge has been laid!'

Scratchy scraped and clawed furiously at the ground, the dust and dirt filling his beak and eyes. There was a ripping and a tearing as the roots of the tiny tree suddenly started to give in to the weight of the massive iron frying pan suspended over the branch. A bit more to go . . . he scratched his sharp claws into the earth once more, and . . .

THUNK!

The pan hit the ground and the blunderbuss went off, blasting smoke and leaves into the air. It wasn't a loud explosion, but it was sudden and unexpected. Bob stumbled backwards in surprise, fumbling with Blasty Bess.

BANG!

In his shock, he fired his own gun into the air.

Smoke billowed across the clearing and a cascade of dead leaves and twigs showered down from the branches overhead.

Everyone screeched at once.

Instinctively, Bob dived for cover. But

it was too late. A great cacophony of cawing and shrieking erupted from the Crow Tree. The deafening racket became a furious cloud of black wings rolling out of the branches like lava. Bob scrambled to his feet but the angry crows were upon him, striking like arrows.

'What was that?!' he shouted, but the others had already started to flee. 'Oi, where are you lot going? Help!'

The crows were outraged. There would be no mercy for the Nasty Faces. They swirled round Bob, jabbing at his arms as he tried to shield himself from the ferocious onslaught. They soared after the other highwaymen, a clamouring uproar of black feathers and snapping beaks. The rallying cry of the crows went out far and wide and was answered with enraged fury, flying in from every direction, obstructing the highwaymen's escape.

Scratchy was shouting *'Mob them! Mob them!'* at the big crows. He leaped and fluttered excitedly as they surged around the Nasty Faces, soaring, tumbling, striking and screaming their triumph.

Bravely, Scratchy flew as fast as he could, low to the ground and steady, straight at the big stinker.

Lil followed up the crows' attack with her slingshot and dumplings.

Most of her missiles missed, but one hit Rotten Bob smack on the rump. He yelped and got his leg tangled in a long straggle of bramble that snaked out of the bushes. He tripped and sprawled to the ground and as he went down, Scratchy swooped in and caught him with an almighty peck, right on the nose. Bob flailed and flapped on the floor.

'No! No! Leave me alone,' he whimpered. Most of the crows had gone storming after the other highwaymen, chasing them through the trees. But a handful of sleek black faces sat in the low branches of the Crow Tree, staring at Bob as he floundered in the leaves.

'*Caw? Caw!*' They squawked and nattered to each other.

Bob looked up at the black beady eyes and sharp dagger-like beaks surrounding him. He started to scuttle away, scooting himself along the floor on his bottom.

One particularly large bird flew down to the ground and hopped closer. '*CAW!*' it croaked menacingly, watching Rotten Bob through one eye, and then the other.

Bob clambered to his feet without taking his eyes off the crow.

It hopped closer again.

There was a great rustling from the bushes as Ghastly Jack loomed into view, huge and ghoulish with an evil grimace on his face, his clawlike finger pointing accusingly.

Bob held his hands up defensively and whittled an apology, 'All right, Ghastly Jack...you win. It...it's your territory. I...I'm leaving now,' he snivelled.

The ghoul took a lumbering step towards him. The crow hopped closer.

'I...I won't come back,' Bob sobbed in a tiny voice.

A big sleek crow stretched out her wings, dipped her powerful beak forward and blasted a piercing '*CAW CAAW CAAAAW!*'

Rotten Bob Hatchet turned with a terrified scream.

He raised his arms over his head and ran shrieking through the trees, stumbling over roots and plunging into the stinging nettles as the great flock of crows dive-bombed him viciously from above.

He was defeated.

26

A Hero

Lil quietly hooked Choakes's cape back over the mounting rail of the coach. He was snoring heartily and she didn't want to wake him. She carried Scratchy back to the turnip shed, stroking his sleek black head.

'Good boy, Scratchy, you saved us all tonight. You are the bravest crow ever!'

'I really thought we was done for. Until Scratchy set off the trap!' whispered Ned. He was carrying the panniers, the frying pan and the blunderbuss.

'I'm sorry I put you in so much danger, Ned. I was stupid. It could have got really nasty out there.'

'It all turned out fine in the end, Lil. I . . . I still feel kind of . . . shaky . . . in a good way! I guess that's what exciting is!'

Lil laughed. 'I think it is! Though I reckon Rotten Bob and his goons could have done with a bit less excitement from the crows.'

'I doubt that lot will be back any time soon. That was great!' Ned was beaming.

Scratchy gave a contented caw as Lil placed him onto the turnip shovel. 'Me and Ned have got to creep back inside and pretend we've been a-bed all night, so sweet dreams, Scratchy, and I'll see you in the morning.'

Scratchy plumped up his feathers, closed his eyes and settled in to roost. Lil could have sworn he was smiling.

At four in the morning, the peace at the inn was shattered by frantic banging on the front door.

Ma wrapped her shawl round her shoulders and stomped into her slippers. 'All right! All right! What time do you think this is?' she bellowed. If anyone had managed to sleep through the door knocking, they were certainly awake now.

Ma flung back the latches and heaved open the door. Two scoundrels stood in the porch, ashen-faced with terror.

'What do you want?' Ma growled.

They nervously explained how they had been chased through the haunted woods by a flock of murderous crows. They were trembling as they babbled about a *demon highwayman*. Ma told them to clear off, but they begged to be allowed inside.

'Don't cast us out into the horrors of the night again, madam!' they implored. 'Here take this, take everything we have, just let us in for heaven's sake, if you have any mercy in you at all!'

Well, Ma didn't have any mercy in her, but she *did* have a whole heap of greed. She seized the purse of coins and weighed it up and down in her hand.

'This all you got, then?' she asked suspiciously, even though it was many times what she'd normally charge for a room for the night.

'Take this an' all then, fair madam, and this, and these,' the highwaymen pleaded, piling watches and trinkets into Ma's grasping hands, 'just *please* let us in off the road on this evil ghost-ridden night!'

Ma snatched the second purse offered to her and peered inside. It was full of gold.

'All right then, in you get.' She pulled them through the door and slammed it behind them. 'Now what's all this nonsense about crows and ghouls? You two been at the spirits?'

The whole household had been woken up, and Lil stood shivering in her nightgown on the stairs.

'Stoke up the fire, Lil. These two gentlemen are shaking,' Ma ordered. 'Now, sit down over there and tell us your story...'

Lil and Ned feigned sleepy innocence.

The highwaymen told their shocking tale of ghastliness and terror to the astonishment of the inn's inhabitants. Everyone was eager for the gory details.

Lil thought she'd encourage things along, saying she'd heard the coachmen talking of similar horrors. Apparently, there was a legend of a hideous, merciless fiend who stalked the highway by night. And even, a neighbour had said he'd heard unearthly moaning in the woods at midnight.

'That's him! Ghastly Jack Crowheart the Demon Highwayman!' The two rascals began jabbering in fright.

As Ma tried to calm them down again, Arthur Boote came rushing in through the back door. 'We're coming!

We're coming!' he yelled. The Bootes had obviously been
woken up by all the door-banging commotion, and Arthur
had hurried over with his breeches on back-to-front to
rescue Margery from the villains. He was surprised to find
her perfectly unharmed, standing in her curlers, serving hot
tea to the guests.

'Do stop making a fuss, Arthur,' Margery chided.
'Anyone would think you were simple in the head! *You*
haven't been chased by a *demon highwayman,* have you?'

Ghastly Jack's Bloomers

Later that morning, as the inn was recovering from the previous night's excitement and scandal, Lil slipped a crust of buttered toast into her apron pocket, while she cleared away the breakfast plates. Scratchy deserved an extra treat today.

Ma was in an exceptionally good mood after last night's windfall. The highwaymen had risen early, eaten a sparse breakfast and hurried out of the inn, explaining they had a long way to go and didn't want to get caught on the road after dark. She flitted between the tables, arranging jars of pickles and crooning to herself cheerfully.

Soon a coach pulled into the stable yard and passengers

got out, chattering about the puddle and the inconvenience of having to stop to fix the axle. They ordered lunch and refreshments and sat in their absurd bonnets awaiting Ma's cooking. Most importantly, they had their purses thoroughly intact, and Ma had wasted no time upselling her rare and particular 'local delicacies'. To Lil's great relief, she seemed to have abandoned all notions of selling the inn. There was no mention of highwaymen.

Mr Sprottle had ventured into the breakfast room too, his appetite apparently having returned to him after spending several days under a tea towel with his nose bent over a steaming bowl of mint.

Ned stood behind him, holding a platter of burned scrambled eggs.

Mr Sprottle regretted having missed Countess Hollingcroft's event in its entirety, but he felt certain that the guests must surely be travelling back this way, and that perhaps the inn itself might serve as a base for operations, for the time being? After a good hour of bargaining, he had agreed to cut Ma into a percentage of his profits, and

she had agreed to let Mr Sprottle distribute his pamphlets about the tables. Lil was delighted at the prospect of having her friend Ned stay for a few weeks longer.

Due to the night-time disturbances at the inn, the legend of Ghastly Jack Crowheart, as told by Lil Scroggins, had spread throughout Eggy Bottom and the neighbouring villages. Margery and Maude gossiped about it all that day, repeating the horrible details of the sailor's plight,

embellishing the romantic bits (his long-lost daughter had somehow been transformed into his long-lost love), and the ghoulish intentions of Ghastly Jack. Arthur made sure everyone knew about the dunking in the ditch bit and the crows pecking out the eyeballs too. The inn was famous!

Lil did have *one* crafty idea for how she might squeeze a little more profit out of the terrifying tale.

She pinned her own polite little notice to the fence along the track on the way to the inn:

For the avoidance of misfortune, travellers are reminded to slip a penny into Ghastly Jack's Bloomers

Never did anyone any harm to take precautions, did it? And it was a good way of keeping Scratchy out of trouble. His menacing presence perched on the gate post tended to encourage folk to pay up.

CAAAW!

The End